WENDELL

THE WORLD'S WORST WIZARD

J.C. SPENCER

Date of First Publication: November 12, 2013

Wren Media
Wren Media Group LLC
P.O. Box 5970
Glendale, AZ 85312
United States of America

ISBN: 9781493658800

Please note:
Any relationship to historical persons is entirely coincidental.

DEDICATION

We dedicate this book to our children, whose imaginations and bedtime stories have been incredible inspiration. May you live courageously with love as your guide. May you always read and always create.

ACKNOWLEDGEMENTS

A special thank you to every person who cheered us on through this entire journey. We want to thank all three of our kids who offered ideas and feedback in the early formation of the story. Also, thank you to Timothy Gwynn and Philip Cummings, who encouraged us to write, illustrate and publish the book. Finally, thank you to Pam Spencer for editing the book.

CONTACT US

Site
jcspencer.us

Facebook
facebook.com/spencerauthor

Twitter
Wendell: @wendellwizard
Author: @spencerauthor

YouTube
youtube.com/spencerauthor

E-mail
info@wendellthewizard.com

CONTENTS

No dragons were harmed in the making of this book.

ONE
I'M NOT EPIC

My full name is Wendell Darrel Drackenberger. I know, I know, it rolls off the tongue like a mouth full of marbles. Just about the worst thing you can give a wizard is a bad name. An oversized puffy pullover? You can fake a smile and save it for an ugly sweater party when you're grown up. An embarrassing haircut? You'll outgrow it, but not a bad name. You're stuck with your name forever.

My friend Michael goes by Mike and Scott goes by Scotty, but what am I supposed to go by? Wind? Wendy? It doesn't work.

I was supposed to be named David. However, on the morning I was born, Mildred Fitz, the village fortune-teller approached my parents and

GREAT GIFTS

The Super Duper Turbo-
Charged Zoom Broom 7.125

A dragon puppy.

A new enchanted
hat with hidden
compartments

CRAPPY GIFTS

A name like Wendell,
Darrell or both.

An ugly sweater.
Yep, I'm calling you out,
Aunt Gertrude.

Two free tickets to Pearl
E. White's Luxury
Dentistry.

said, "His name shall be Wendell and he will go on to do amazing and wonderful things."

"Wow, *amazing* and *wonderful*? Isn't that redundant?" my dad asked.

"Ahem," she went on, "Thus begins from this very hour, the boy at once will switch the power. Our world will be plagued by bitter darkness and he will rise up from the starkness. So now I stand as your predictor, this very child will be our victor."

Now, what those bitter dark things were, she didn't specify. Fortune-tellers tend to work in the abstract. My mom took the prophecy seriously and named me Wendell. Then, just in case she hadn't listened correctly, she added Darrell as a middle name.

The name alone should have raised a red flag. Have you ever known a hero named Wendell? Think about it. Just one. That's right. You can't, because heroes aren't named Wendell.

The next day, it came out that Mildred had been drunk. Apparently, she told this same prophecy to every mother whose child was born that day. Okay, that's not entirely true. By the ninth baby, she was so drunk that her prediction was, "You're going to have an amazing and wonderful windowsill and it will save you from darkness." Curt and Rod's Window Dressing Shop had never experienced so much business in one day.

Mildred lost her fortune-telling license. Stripped of all prediction powers, she opened a modest snow cone shop at the local cemetery. She's won Best Enchanted Snow Cone three out of the last four years. She has a snow cone cannon charmed to shoot ice in the air and land perfectly in a cup.

Mildred's prophecy wasn't just wrong; it was totally, completely and utterly wrong. I realized all of this on Wand Wielding Wednesday, the first official day for witches and wizards to learn incantations.

I was an eager seven year old, trying to imagine what it would be like to transform objects with the flip of the wrist. Maybe I'd turn Greg's favorite hat into a pair of old socks. Then I would suddenly "find" the hat and he would have to be nice to me for a day. Or better yet, I could transform broccoli into taffy when my parents weren't looking.

My Great Grandma Drackenberger (who I always call "grandma," because she's the only grandparent who lives near us) met me at Smells Like Bundt, the finest bakery in all of Bezaudorf (our enchanted village). It's a weekly Wednesday tradition.

Betty Bundt, being a firt (a non-magical wizard), struggled to open a cabinet where a knob had popped off.

Mr. Buchanan, head of the Bank on the Bank (and father to Bruno the Ballistic Bully Boy) started tapping his foot. He huffed gigantic sighs and pulled out his pocket watch to prove a point.

"You're tap dancing all wrong. This is a slow song," my grandma said, pointing to the self-playing accordion snoozing in the corner.

He rolled his eyes while Betty continued wrestling with the cabinet.

"No, no, no. It's a slow song. You're tapping all wrong," my grandma said, tapping her feet to the beat. "This is the right tempo."

"This frumpy firt can't figure out a simple cabinet!" he yelled loud enough to rouse the accordion. Red-faced, he continued, "She doesn't even belong in our world. Dirty and disenchanted. There was a time when we wouldn't have tolerated this."

My grandma shook her head. "You need to cool off. Take an Icy Mint," she muttered, holding out her hand.

He huffed and turned away.

She tapped him on the shoulder. "Take it. You'll cool off . . . literally." She was right at the time. The original Icy Mints could form crystals along your tongue. They had to change the charm after wizards who weren't paying attention ended up at the apothecary for freezer burns.

"I don't want your candy! What I want is a sticky bun and this incompetent imbecile can't get it right."

"Suit yourself." She tossed the mint in her mouth. Seconds later, she belched out a stream of flames that singed Mr. Buchanan's perfectly pressed robes.

"Oops. I think it was a fireball."

"What was that for?" he asked.

"I'm so old and senile I get confused. These candies all look the same," she said, shrugging her shoulders.

As he turned around, she pulled out her walking stick (which was really just a staff attached to the wand she had to get rid of when she was deemed "too old for wand wielding") and sent a stack of sticky buns flying toward his face.

"You! You did that!" he screamed, pulling chunks of caramel out of his nostrils.

She shrugged her shoulders again.

"I saw it! That stupid walking stick of yours. It's enchanted!"

"I'm just a senile old lady." She said as she sauntered toward the counter and filled the tip jar to the brim.

"And here's a tip for you, Mr. Buchanan, you're supposed to pay for your pastries *before* you eat them." Mr. Buchanan left the shop covered in caramel. While my grandma walked behind the counter and fixed the knob, Betty brought out a super-deluxe, extra frosting cinnamon roll.

Minutes later, Grandma Drackenberger pulled out a shiny box. The unicorn sketches pranced off the wrapping paper in a blast of color.

"Go on," she implored.

I wiped my fingers on my robe and tore apart the paper (much to the dismay of the falling unicorns). It wasn't just a wand. It was a first-class, solid maple, silver-tipped Sanderling Ultra.

I slid it out of the box and twirled it in the air. She swatted at my hand. "Careful. Don't want to poke an eye out. You've got a lot to learn first. You know the prophecy. You're supposed to be great."

The door burst open and my friend Sarah Bellum (an equally bad name) waved her wand in the air. "I did that, Wendell. I did that with this."

"Ims urt thime?" I asked, my mouth full of frosting.

"Digs art time?" Sarah asked.

I cleared my throat. "Is it time?"

"Yeah!" she yelled as she pulled me out of my seat. Together, we raced through the Town Tetrahedron and headed toward the school, our minds swimming with the shared visions of a first day of magic.

An hour later, I sat in a crowded lecture hall listening to Mr. Oglesby explain all the ways we could lose a limb. It was supposed to encourage safety, but I had a hunch that Bruno was getting some new ideas instead.

I pulled out my brand-new wand, concentrated on the coins we were supposed to transform and flicked my wrist just like our teacher demonstrated. Nothing happened. I tried it again. And again. Still nothing.

CHAPTER ONE

One-by-one, my classmates were turning their copper coins into gold, but mine wouldn't even change color.

"Let's try it with a training wand. Perhaps the Sanderling Ultra is too much for a child," my teacher said.

Again, nothing happened. I tried two more training wands to no avail.

Finally, on my last try, I aimed at the coins and all five turned to gold.

"It worked. I did it," I called out to Sarah.

However, I knew something was wrong when I heard Bruno the Ballistic Bully Boy cackling.

"That was a mean trick," Sarah snarled. Without warning, she whispered a string-tying charm on Bruno's shoes. He tripped on his way out the door and face-planted on the stone floor.

Things felt better in Levitations, where I lifted a tomato and placed it inches above a boiling cauldron.

"Nicely done, Mr. Drackenberger. Just like your brothers," my teacher pointed out. I glanced over to Bruno's surprised face. Clearly, he wasn't holding a wand. It had to be me.

Yet as he turned away, the tomato dropped into the cauldron. I waved my wand. I concentrated as hard as I could. Still, it didn't work. I tried it on two new tomatoes.

That's when I realized that Bruno had been hiding his wand inside his robe.

The next three classes moved by with a stream of "I don't know what's wrong" and "There's never been an issue with a Drackenberger before."

When I arrived home, my mom met me at the door with a sympathetic glance. "I have a surprise for you," she said.

Our family walked to the graveyard (not exactly a typical place for a surprise) where we met Mildred the Former Fortune Teller.

"The pups are just old enough to adopt," she explained.

I knelt down in the grass as Mildred droned on about their lineage. "They're from the Lee family of dragons. Though, their roots are the Norman Du Lea family. So, you're dealing with purebreds."

Having so many dragons in one place, her home smelled like barbecued ribs. I guess that's what you get when your pets can flame-broil their own dinner.

I studied Fierce Lee, the crimson-colored dragon with a scowl to match his sharp horns. It could be nice to have a dragon defender to stand up to Bruno the Ballistic Bully Boy.

Then it was the pudgy Lazy Lee, a gentle dragon that licked my hands with his forked tongue.

"Fork-tongued puppy kisses tickle, huh?" Mildred pointed out.

A dragon darted past me, whipping my back with her tail.

"That's Swift Lee. She's already flying," Mildred said. "It would be nice to have such a fast learner," my dad pointed out.

"She won't need to be de-flamed, either. She's already learned not to flame on command."

With each of the dragons clamoring for attention, I stepped away and pointed to a runt of a pup.

"What's her name?"

Mildred shook her head. "I'm sorry, Wendell. She's not supposed to be here right now. She must have snuck out somehow."

"Well, what's her name?" I repeated.

"Sweetheart, that dragon isn't supposed to . . . oh, my, well . . . you explain," my mom said, gesturing to my dad.

"Well, um," my dad sputtered out, "she can't fly, Wendell. She never will. She's scrawny and weak and she probably won't make it. I don't want you to get attached just to find out that she's sickly."

I would love to say that she bonded with me on the spot, but she didn't. Instead, she cowered in the corner and whimpered. She ducked when I offered my hand.

"Please don't. For the love of Merlin, look at the other dragons instead," my mom begged.

Still, I tried to figure out a name. She was a dull gray, like dirty concrete. "How about Ash? I guess that would make her Ash Lee." I said.

"Oh, I don't know," my dad said, stroking his beard. "She'll break your heart, Wendell."

But it was too late. The pathetic pup hobbled into my arms and nudged my neck. That was it. She became our dragon. No, that's not right. She became *my* dragon and she still is.

For the next six years, I tried my hardest to conjure up magic. I memorized the spells and learned to use different accents with the hopes that maybe if I sounded slightly Scottish the wand would work. I saved up my allowance money and bought a specialized wand from Wanda's Wand Em*power*ium. When that failed, I tried to tame my wandering mind. Nothing worked.

Magic is like that. You're either born with it or you're not and at thirteen years old, it is pretty clear that I'm a firt.

The truth is that I have it good for a firt. I have a few close friends and no one expects too much from me. Besides, I have a dragon as a roommate. How cool is that?

I promise that this will not just be a sad story about a kid who can't do magic that mopes around his castle complaining about his life. There will be action and adventure, a few robots, some zombies, at least one troll and a gnome. However, it doesn't start out that way. No, it starts out on the eve of the worst day of my life.

WHY I'M NOT EPIC

Way too short to be a hero.

A mind that daydreams about making things.

I can't wield a wand to save my life . . . or anyone else's.

My 20/20 vision means I won't be getting dignified wizard spectacles.

Scared eyes

My robe looks like a cape, because I never tie it correctly.

My clothes are covered in much from being thrown into cauldrons.

People call me Dragon Booger. Nice.

Most un-heroic name ever.

WENDELL DARRELL DRACKENBERGER

TWO
BENNY'S BIG SECRET

The truth is that I've managed to make it through most of my non-magical days just fine because of a tiny secret. I make stuff. I don't magic it together. I connect it with my hands and a few choice tools.

It doesn't always work. Okay, it almost never works. However, on the occasion that it does, it feels like magic. I take my parchment and ink idea and turn it into reality and it feels, for a moment, like I can conquer the universe.

Today, though, I'm not looking to conquer the universe. I just need a couple of gears and a pulley for a robot I'm making. Someday I want to make a robot that will move on its own.

I stop by Mildred's place to pick up smuggled goods from the DUMP. The DUMP is the term for the non-magical world. It stands for Disenchanted and Unable to do Magic Place.

We call it smuggling, but it's technically not illegal. It's more of an unspoken law that DUMP items are un-wizardly and not worth owning. My parents would kill me if they knew about my robots.

Mildred went underground years ago. Literally. She has a home inside a grassy mound with a back door that connects to a complex system of tunnels that she uses to transport disenchanted goods.

She meets me at the door with a mug of hot chocolate. "Sit by the fire," she says. Not that I need to get warmer. If disenchanted neighborhoods have the "crazy cat lady," we have the "crazy dragon lady." With seven of them breathing in one tiny space, you don't really need a fireplace.

I sit next to Swift Lee and scratch her snout. It's warm enough for my hot chocolate to bubble. Even though I have a nagging sense that there's something I need to do, I sit down on her blackened couch and brush off the stray dragon fur.

"So, tomorrow's the big day," Mildred says.

"I'm going to be humiliated," I admit.

"You will go on to do great and, what was it I said? Amazing. Yes, amazing things. Or maybe wonderful. Either way, this is just a test."

I shake my head. I know how the LAME test works. They put you in a room, one-on-one, and drill you on spells before giving your score to the various magic academies before the Invitation Ceremony.

Mildred pulls a large marshmallow out of cupboard, sets it on a stick and shuffles over to Slow Lee. "Hey boy, breathe." The dragon stretches, yawns and spews out just enough flames to roast the marshmallow.

"Now that right there - a perfectly browned marshmallow - that's magical. Want it?"

I shake my head. I don't want to eat. The truth is I don't really want to drink hot chocolate, either. I'd like to jump forward a few days and be done with the LAME test and the Invitation Ceremony.

THREE REASONS IT SUCKS TO BE A FIRT

I can't pay for things with my wand, which means a long line gathers behind me every time I need to make change.

Most wizards open doors with their wands, which means the handles are decorative at best. So, I'm either locked out or I end up breaking the door.

I am the last one chosen whenever we play schnorbitz, an enchanted disk game that requires a wand and a pegasus.

BUT DO I COMPLAIN?
WELL, YEAH, SOMETIMES.
BUT NOT AS MUCH AS YOU'D THINK.

"Wendell, it's not the end of the world if you turn out to be a firt."

"Um, it kind-of is," I mutter.

"Are you sure it's not your wand? Sometimes the workers at Wanda's Wand Em*power*ium toss some oak twigs in with a batch so they don't fall behind on their quotas. That's what happened to me. I grew up believing I was a firt when I was really just putzing around with nothing more than a dud. Maybe you need a replacement wand."

"Nope. I've been through almost twenty of them," I point out.

"Well, it was worth a shot." She sighs and twirls the marshmallow. "You know, I was a firt on my evaluation day."

"How'd it go?"

"They played a prank on me. A wizard snuck in and charmed the cauldron. For a second, I thought I was really magical. But then it stopped. Wizards can be cruel to misfits."

I nod.

"Well, I could always use an apprentice. If you can't get into a school, you could work for me," she says.

"And learn the art of snow cone making?"

She laughs and slaps me on the back, her marshmallow hands sticking to my robe. "You could be a smuggler, Wendell. You'd be perfect for it. No one would suspect you."

"Isn't the DUMP disgusting?"

She shakes her head. "The DUMP is a beautiful place. They have these things called microwaves that are twenty times faster than cauldrons. You'd love it."

"My parents wouldn't."

"Well, there is that, I suppose," she says. "But it beats working as a dragon groomer's assistant."

"That's what I was supposed to do!" I slam the mug down and run to the door.

"What's the hurry?"

"I haven't given Ash a wingcut this month and my mom thinks she's going to fly away."

"She can't fly."

"I know. But try telling my mom that," I mumble as I brace for the icy wind outside the cozy mound.

I run across the frosty grass and head down the cobblestone road of the Town Tetrahedron, taking the shortcut past the dancing motion pictures of Lucero's Cinema and past the crowds at Noah's Arcade (where you get a discount when you enter two-by-two).

With the daylight fading, I jump over Benny's tiny fence. I mean, it's a decent sized fence for a gnome, but for me it's more like a tiny hurdle.

CAN YOU SPOT THE DIFFERENCE?

If you live next to a bearded guy who likes funny hats and has a real knack for gardening, chances are you are neighbors with a gnome. Unless you're in Portland, where it's impossible to tell the difference.

Unlike gnomes, elves can't grow beards. Oh yeah, and their ears are pointy. However, behind the constant grin is a sharp mind, able to design just about anything.

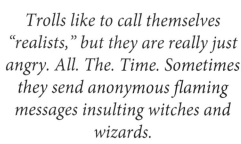

Trolls like to call themselves "realists," but they are really just angry. All. The. Time. Sometimes they send anonymous flaming messages insulting witches and wizards.

BROUGHT TO YOU BY THE COUNCIL OF COUNSEL

I jog through his immaculate backyard, but as I reach his patio, there's a deafening crash. I step back. Did I break something? His potted plants remain intact. Everything is in a tidy row.

I take a deep breath, but as I turn around, I notice one final pot teetering on the edge. I wrap my hands around the base, but it won't budge. I pull harder this time. Nothing happens. I pause and listen to a faint creaking sound growing louder by the second.

"Benny?" I ask.

That's when I see it. The floorboards are shifting around like puzzle pieces. Suddenly, I'm holding on to the porch rail and doing the splits. A chasm opens up. My legs shake. Below me, a staircase appears. I pull myself out of the splits and stand on the first step.

"Benny? Are you there?" Nothing.

"I think I broke something of yours. Maybe your patio?"

Still no answer. I step forward and look back. I could walk away. If someone broke into his basement, no one would know I had opened the secret passage.

"Hey Benny," I yell down the steps. "I accidentally opened this up and . . ."

A door slams above me followed by the clicking of a double bolt. I let out a yelp. Flames flicker on in the lamps around me. Heart hammering, I tiptoe along the stairs and duck down in the cramped-up basement.

"Definitely gnome-sized," I mutter, unable to stand up straight. The room is packed full of boxes with large black letters reading, "DUMP." I look both ways and open a box. It's filled with thin colored strings. A neatly written note card reads, "Miscellaneous wiring." I'm not sure what "wiring" is, but I have to hand it to Benny. Anyone who can spell *miscellaneous* correctly has to be pretty bright.

Another box reads, "Random Yard Sale." I can't imagine they can fit a whole yard into a box. Then again, he's a gnome and they tend to figure out the space compression spells pretty quickly. Maybe that's his secret landscaping technique. He goes to the disenchanted and buys their yards and then decompresses one when a wizard needs a new lawn.

Other items don't seem so lawn-oriented. There are boxes with buttons and knobs and coils. Here I've been going to Mildred for robot parts and all I ever needed to do was walk across the street to Benny's cottage.

When I glance at the metal boxes and the strings popping out of each side, I can't help but feel like he's making robots of his own.

I meander over to a dusty table and pull up the stool. I flip through the stack of papers where I find an envelope on weathered parchment.

The curling cursive letters float above my face. I can't make out the words. Something about payback and respect and avenging a dart. No, it can't be a dart. A death, maybe? I flip it over and notice a jagged square. As I brush my hand against it, an emerald emblem emerges.

I recognize it instantly. It can't be. Not Benny. Not the quiet, happy garden gnome from across the street. Not the architect of the greatest gingerbread houses known to wizardkind. It's impossible. He's the sweetest guy in the all of Bezaudorf. Literally. He grows his own cotton candy and uses it to knit floating edible party confetti. The logo fades back into the dark. I brush my hand against it again. Clearly, it's the seal of the Misfits.

The door bursts open.

"Wendell?"

I squeal like a band of pixies in a hailstorm.

"Melissa?" he asks.

"Nope, it's Wendell." Apparently, I sound like my sister when I scream.

"What did you see?" he asks.

"Nothing. I didn't see anything at all," I lie.

"This is a private room," he says. "You're welcome to stop by any time. You can have some peppermint pie. But this room is off limits. There are things in here that are dangerous."

My whole body shakes. "I . . . I . . . um . . . I need to give my dragon a . . ."

"You look scared," he says.

"I'm sorry," I say.

He snaps his finger. "Say, do you want a little advantage on your evaluations tomorrow?"

"I'm not magical," I admit.

"But you could be mechanical." He rips open a box and starts tossing items across the room. "We could fix you a wand. A wireless wand. Then again, I suppose all wands are wireless. But, yes, it just might work. Wendell, stop by tomorrow morning. I'll make you a wand that might earn you some points on the LAME test."

I shake my head. "I need to go."

"Listen, if you make it into a mid-level school, you won't need magic. You can fake it. I could help you. Then you can become a Maker. Wouldn't you like to design things? I suspect you already have."

"How do you know?" I ask.

"I know more than you think. Honestly, I'm worried about you. I don't want you going Filbert on us."

"I won't. I promise." I jog home. Before I can bang on the door, a mobile message flies toward me and lands on my shoulders. It's from the Misfits. I guess Benny isn't the only one thinking that I'll go Filbert on Bezaudorf.

Are you an elf that can't manage to make a single enchanted object?

Are you a witch that can't use a wand?

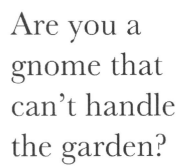

Are you a gnome that can't handle the garden?

THE MISFITS
You now have a voice.

Fighting for integration
of firts and other
"non-magical" folk.

Fighting for equal rights
within the entire
enchanted world..

Fighting for the
right to use
any enchanted
tool.

THREE
THE LAMEST L.A.M.E. TEST EVER

As I turn down the wrong corridor, Big Bruno Buchanan the Ballistic Bully Boy yells, "Hey Dragon Booger Boy. You won't get picked. You know that, right?"

I ignore him.

"I'm talking to you, Dragon Booger. You know what's going to happen. If you screw this up, you'll get no banners. You know that, right?"

I ignore him again. He steps in front of me, blocking the corridor.

"You know why, right?" he asks again.

Okay. So much for ignoring him.

"I'm a firt," I say.

"Yeah, and you know why they call you a *fart*? Because you stink at magic."

His minion, Joe, steps in, "Actually, you know who can do less magic than Dragon Booger?"

"Who?" Bruno asks.

"Nobody."

Bruno barely cracks a smile. I step back, hoping this is the end of it.

"I can't wait to see the silence when they call your name," Bruno adds.

"You don't really *see* silence," I correct him. "It's more of something you hear. Or don't hear, I guess."

He pulls out his wand and aims it at my throat.

"I'm sorry. I'm sorry," I plead.

"Don't worry," he says. "I wouldn't do anything to you today. I want to see you get embarrassed tonight."

He'll get his chance, too. All three of my older brothers were chosen for the elite Fancy Shmancy Magical Academy for Great and Awesome and Even Occasionally Terrible Wizards. It's a bad name, but a great school. They take you in a flying chariot with gold-plated hubcaps, carried along by pegasae (not one pegasus, but four pegasae).

I'm not sure I agree on the pegasus choice. It's supposed to sound dignified, but have you seen a flying horse? It's not all that dignified when they start dropping their droppings from three hundred feet in the air. It's downright dangerous. The Safety Committee has been lobbying for years for a simple pooper-scooper at the end, but the school doesn't want to mess with tradition. They say it's not dignified (as if a half pound of pegasus poop falling from the air is somehow better).

For what it's worth, Bruno keeps his word. He doesn't toss me into the dirty cauldrons. He doesn't levitate my hat just inches above where I can jump.

The truth is that he looks kind-of nervous about this afternoon. Even the bullies are worried about passing the LAME test (Limited Assessment of Magical Enchantments) this afternoon and attending the Invitation Ceremony tonight.

TRANSPORTATION METHODS OF ENCHANTED SCHOOLS

The Fancy Shmancy Magical Academy for Great and Awesome and Even Occasionally Terrible Wizards uses pegasae. You fly your way to school. Pretty nice.

The Zimdorfska Academy prefers unicorn rides through an enchanted forest. Sounds great until you realize that unicorns are easily distracted by wildflowers and pixies. It makes for a long ride.

The Pretty Good Discount School for the Mostly-Magical Kids sends witches and wizards on canoes through a magical underground waterway called "the sewer." It's fun, but occasionally they run into giant mutated tortoises that do ninja.

I spend the afternoon tapping my quill and trying to imagine how I'll handle the LAME test. I'm already regretting the decision not to stop by Benny's and pick up a secret gadget. I know, I know, he might be working with the Misfits. However, I wouldn't mind some kind of an edge.

I move through the day like a boy waiting to be punched in the gut. Mrs. Meaniebobeanie's lesson on author's purpose feels purposeless (it's the last day of school). Mr. Snodgray's lesson on the Great Elf Insurrection feels anything but great. Even Mr. Thompson's lab on forces and motion feels forced and motionless. For all the talk of acceleration, time itself seems to decelerate.

Finally, it happens. We meet in the lecture hall and wait for our names to be called. Sarah's the only one who doesn't seem nervous. Then again, she doesn't have to be nervous. She can out-magic anyone in our school.

Eventually, they call my name. I gulp and walk toward the hallway. An ancient lady meets me with a scowl. Her hat and clothes are so dusty it looks like she might decompose right there in the corridor.

"Hat off. Let's keep this classy," she barks.

"Okay," I say.

"Ma'am."

"Oh, I'm not a ma'am. I'm a boy. Wait, you were correcting me, weren't you?"

She nods. "We shall start with the easy enchantments. Please make this quill float."

I wave my wand and breathe out as hard as I can. The feather flutters.

"Ahem, please perform the spell."

I try it again.

She scowls at me. "Excuse me, but that didn't move."

"Oh, it moved. Just not very high," I point out. I do it twice more, but she shakes her head and scribbles notes on her parchment.

"On your application, you listed walking on water. Would you like to go to the lake in order to demonstrate this phenomenon?"

"It only works when it's frozen," I point out. She raises an eyebrow.

"Or if it just rained. But then it's walking *in* water instead of *on* water, I guess."

Her scowl turns into a death stare. I decide to come clean. "Most of the skills are kind-of exaggerated."

"I'll take note of that when I meet with the committee." She scribbles a few more notes on her scroll. The room is edgy. I consider breaking the tension by breaking wind, but I have a hunch she wouldn't like it all that much.

Instead, I limit myself to a burp. It starts small, but it doesn't stop. Next thing I know, I'm belching out the alphabet and I'm all the way at Q, so I might as well make it to Z.

"I give that an eight point three nine," she says, almost cracking a smile. "Nevertheless, I'm afraid we can't count it as magical. It's a shame, too. I'm quite fond of musical burps. Now, let's walk you through some of the more remedial incantations."

As the test moves on, I shrug my shoulders at each request. The stern-faced lady smiles. Not a cruel grin, either, but a real smile.

"That's right. You're a Drackenberger. What do you say we start again? Don't be nervous. You'll be fine. Your brothers were the same way at first and then, well, each one was amazing in different ways."

"Well, I'm a little different than my brothers," I say. "You'll see."

"Like I said, each wizard is different. I look forward to whatever it is you've whipped up for me." Whipped up? She talks about it like I'm baking a cake.

She continues, "Why, I wish you could have seen what Greg was able to do. He transformed my quill into a snake just to see my reaction. I hadn't been that startled in years. It was impressive. Now, why don't you choose the first incantation?"

I shake my head.

"Ahem. Why don't you just tell me what you're good at?"

"I, um, I'm pretty good at making stuff."

"Go on, then. Conjure up something. You've got a cauldron right there and we have a shelf of items to transform if you'd prefer that."

"No, I mean, by hand. I like to design things."

"Like an elf?" She raises an eyebrow.

"I guess. I've been making stuff since I was tiny. I've read every book we have on physics and forces and stuff. I spend every spare minute in my room making stuff."

"Without magic?"

"Yeah, I guess."

"I see," she mutters. "Well, can you make something happen here in this cauldron?"

I shake my head. As the test continues, she realizes that I'm a firt. Her expression moves from stern to disappointed to slightly sad.

She sets the quill down and says, "You can go," before the exam is even over.

CHAPTER THREE

I leave the room with watery eyes. When Sarah asks about it, I lie. "You have to chop onions with only a wand and then levitate each piece into a boiling hot cauldron."

Next, I meet with Mr. Oglesby, the admissions counselor. "We need to talk about your future career goals. As you know, your career aspirations will help you find the right fit for your ideal enchanted academy." He clears his throat. "Ahem, that is, if you get into one."

I nod.

"So, what would you like to do?" he asks.

"I was thinking of being a Designer or maybe a Maker. Ever since I was a little kid, I loved to build stuff. So, I thought maybe I could get into that."

He laughs. Not a chuckle, but a full-scale belly laugh. Then, clearing his throat, he adds, "Sorry, I thought you were joking."

"No, I just thought that, you know, I have some great design ideas. Seeing as how I can't really do magic, I thought I might work on a design team and . . ."

"That's elf work. They have those cute little hands that are perfectly suited for that work." He wiggles his fingers. "You're little, but not little enough."

"I just thought that maybe a human could work with them. I'm pretty good at making stuff. I can do everything but the magic."

"You know what happened with Benny, don't you?"

I nod. You can't live across the street with someone like that and never hear the legend. See, Benny was a gnome who showed high aptitudes for designing things. So, the elves put him in charge of designing a new line of toy dragons. When they said "make it realistic," Benny charmed the toys to fly around and spew fire, leading to a massive workshop fire. Next, they put him in charge of designing "smelly" markers. Unfortunately, he decided to make markers that smelled like vomit, wet dog and "my shirt after a three hour jog." To gnomes, those are all great smells. Unfortunately, witches and wizards disagreed.

"You know, you could always work with the trolls. They make things by hand. Well, they destroy things by hand most of the time, but sometimes they make things. You wouldn't need a wand for it."

"That's an option," I say, but I know trolls. They launch flaming anonymous notes at wizards and scream insults at you when you least expect it.

I lean forward. "What if . . . what if I went out there?"

"To the DUMP?" he asks.

"It was just an idea," I say.

Benny didn't last long with the elves. It's a good thing he redeemed himself by stopping Filbert.
"No. I mean, yeah. Well, maybe." I sputter.

"That's a horrible idea. Do you know how disgusting the DUMP is?"

"Yes, sir."

He adjusts his glasses and peers down at me. "You're not going to go Filbert on us are you?"

"Um, no sir," I shake my head. "I just figured that if I'm not magical, I might fit in better over in their world."

"You're a wizard. Magical or not, you belong here. And there are splendid opportunities for firts." Splendid? Really? Who uses that term?

"I know. I was just curious about it, that's all. I thought maybe I could be a Designer on that side."

He shakes his head. "That's a really bad idea. Choose a nice, quiet life. Stay in Bezaudorf. Figure out how to go unnoticed and you'll be fine. The way I see it, you have an advantage. No one expects anything of you."

FOUR
ASH LEE'S MISTAKE AND OTHER MINOR CATASTROPHES

I walk home with my head hung low. Nobody notices. The whole village is buzzing about the Invitation Ceremony. Note that "Invitation Ceremony" is never written with lowercase letters. To do so would be a capital offense. After all, it's a proper noun and a proper ceremony, complete with dress robes and dragons and glitter bombs that explode in song and dance just inches above the audience; which is exactly what they need after the long list of names and banners and polite clapping for all three hundred students.

"Drackenberger," Benny calls out from his tiny lawn.

I nod.

He jogs toward me, his robe snagging on the underbrush. "You didn't stop by this morning."

"It wouldn't have made a difference."

"Was it that bad?" he asks.

"Worse than I thought it would be."

"Well, if things don't turn out well for you, I have an offer." He hands me a dusty envelope. "You can be my apprentice. Here's an official invitation."

"Well, um, thanks," I say, though I have no desire to work for a yard gnome, or, as he calls it, a "landscape artist."

He points at me. "One more thing: If I were you, I'd avoid the ceremony tonight."

"I don't think my parents will let me," I point out.

He tugs on my robes. "I'm not sure it's safe for you."

"I'll keep that in mind," I mumble as I walk toward our castle and bang on the door. My dad wants to put in a doorknob, but my mom thinks it would "send the wrong message."

I bang on the door again.

"In a second!" my brother Greg yells.

I step back and run toward the door. He opens it right as I summersault into the desk, knocking over the typewriter.

"You ruined my mobile message!" Greg screams. "And you got my robes dirty."

WHY IT SUCKS WHEN MY BROTHER COMES BACK HOME

Greg hogs the typewriter and sends mobile messages back to his girlfriend the whole time.

He takes my bedroom (which is his "old room") and drools on my sheets and snores all night.

He purposely shuts the doors, places things on high shelves and reminds me non-stop that I can't do magic.

He eats all of our food. So, I'm stuck with things like salad instead.

Just to taunt me, he's decided to wear his robes from the Fancy Shmancy Magical Academy for Great and Awesome and Even Occasionally Terrible Wizards.

"I'm sorry," I say, walking toward the kitchen table. Without thinking, I swat away a flittering mobile message.

"Seriously! I'm trying to have a conversation here," he snarls. I walk toward the cauldron. It's empty.

"You ate all the soup," I point out, but Greg turns his back and bangs away at the typewriter, letting the letters fly out the window and zoom toward his girlfriend back at the academy.

"Hey, I said you ate all the soup."

"You are quite observant. Maybe you should be a detective. I mean, seeing as how you can't do any magic, it might be a nice job."

I clench my fists. "What am I supposed to eat?"

He rolls his eyes. "Look, it's not like you could have warmed the soup up anyway. You can't even do a heating charm. Get a salad or something."

"I can't. It'll give me gas and I'm right up by the dragons." Though I'm doubtful about the physics of flammable farts, I don't want to test it tonight.

"It would be a show. The audience would love it," he says. "They'd probably think it was the Misfits attacking."

"That's not funny."

"You know, the sad part is that even the Misfits wouldn't want you," he says. "You're too much of a misfit for the Misfits."

I turn away and bound up the stairs. "Don't mess with my stuff!" Greg yells. Looks like I'll be giving up my room for a week and sleeping in my tiny old bedroom down the hall. As I reach the door, I notice a silky pink dress shirt.

"Mom, where's my dress shirt?" I yell down the echoing hallway.

"It's right there," she says, pointing to it.

"But that's pink."

"Well, your brother's red robe accidentally made it in with the white clothes." I'm having a hard time believing it was truly an accident.

"I can't wear it," I protest.

"Nonsense. You'll look dashing," she says with a smile.

"It's pink."

"Think of it more as light red. You'll be the only wizard with a light red shirt."

Suddenly, the smell of smoke fills my bedroom. I rush toward Ash Lee.

"Bad dragon!"

She ducks her head and drops my dress robe.

"Sweetheart, that's what happens when you leave your robe out all day. I told you to put it away."

"No. No. No. I had my outfit hanging out so it wouldn't get wrinkled. And that worthless . . ."

Ash Lee whimpers.

"Sorry, girl. I just. It's full of holes and . . . why can't we just get her de-flamed like everybody else?"

"That would be cruel," my mom replies. "What if she gets lost and has to make it on her own?"

"It's not like she can fly away. She's not going to get lost."

"Speaking of which," my dad joins as he steps into my doorway, "you haven't clipped her wings this month. I'm afraid she's going to fly away."

"She can't fly. She's not going anywhere."

"Just like you! You won't be going anywhere after tonight!" Greg yells from downstairs.

"Ignore him. You'll do fine tonight. You're smart and kind and creative. I'm guessing . . ."

"I failed the examinations," I interrupt.

"You might be surprised, Wendell," he says, walking backward down the hall. "Some of the schools have lowered their standards in recent years. They might just let you in." I watch the bald spot on his head bob the rest of the way down the stairs.

My mom pipes up from the study, "Besides, we've got a party planned for you. I bet you'll be covered in banners. You're our future hero."

To this day, my mom still believes Mildred's farfetched prophecy. However, that's my mom. She holds onto hope when it's way past its expiration date, stockpiling it by the case, just in case. If you told her that today was the end of the world, she would smile and say, "Well, that's nice. I hope the world has a happy ending."

An hour later, we gather outside Grand Stan's Grandstands. There's a general murmur of "What kind of broom will you get for graduation?" and "I wonder if we get to work with the dragons" and "What if I don't make it to a good school?" and "Are we supposed to call them teachers, professors or masters?" For many of my classmates, this will be the first time they've ever left Bezaudorf.

I'm shivering, as much from nerves as from my wholly holey robe in the chilly air. It doesn't help that I left my hat at home. Bruno seizes the opportunity to say, "It's okay, because only *real* wizards should wear enchanted hats."

He's right. A magic hat will warm the head, defend against curses and transform into a helmet when riding a broom. However, it uses the natural magic inside each wizard. For me, it's more like a fancy decoration.

The weatherman tried to warm it up, but an incantation can only go so far against the earth's tilt. I huddle close to a wheezing dragon. It helps, but I'm still shivering uncontrollably.

Sarah approaches me with a grin. "Nice shirt."

"It's not my fault. My mom washed it on accident with the red clothes and she didn't have time to apply a bleaching charm. She said I could go with it and just call it light red."

"Yeah, well it's pink. Really pink. Here, let me just . . . let me do a bleaching charm." She pulls out her school-issued training wand, flicks her wrist and says, "*Convertis Albis.*"

I look down at my shirt. It's white all right. Bright white, in fact. But then it happens. Pink polka dots emerge throughout the shirt.

"Sorry. I should have gone with a rhyming charm instead of a Latin one. Here, let me fix it," she says, aiming her training wand at my shirt.

"No, no. It's okay," I tell her.

As she flicks her wand, my shirt turns pink with big black polka dots. She offers to fix the mistake, but I'm worried I'll end up with a hot pink robe to match it.

I pull her aside from the crowd. "I think I know someone who's connected to the Misfits."

"Who?"

"Benny. I saw a letter and some . . . stuff . . . from, you know, the DUMP."

Sarah shakes her head. "Benny was a hero. He took out Filbert."

"I guess that's true," I admit, "but I have a hunch he's going to attack tonight. He warned me to stay away from the ceremony."

"You'll be fine. Remember, you don't need a bunch of banners. All you need is one to end up at a school."

I shake my head and pull out a note from my sister. She's six years old and yet she can do more magic in a day than I have done in my lifetime.

Deer Wendill,

Good luck. You'll do grate. I hope you get like a hundred gazilian banners and they rap you up like a rainbow.

Love, Melissa.

She sketches a picture of a flying chariot. It floats off the page the instant I open the card. As I re-read her note, I notice Bruno batting away at the flittering motion picture. I smile as I imagine myself carried away by the chariot, shocking the village that never saw me as anything more than a firt.

FIVE
THE INVITATION CEREMONY

Every student is anxious. That's a given. For most of them it's the same nervous anticipation they feel on Christmas. For me it's a little different. It's more like the moment I arrive at Dr. Pearl E. White's Luxury Dentistry with a toothache and I'm not sure how bad it's going to be.

I know that I haven't done anything wrong, but still I wonder about it. What if I wasn't born this way? What if I had believed with more intensity when I said the spells? What if I hadn't built stuff with items from the DUMP?

Memories race across my mind. Was it the time I jumped off the bunk bed and hit my head on the chandelier? The extra spoonfuls of sugar behind my mom's back? Perhaps the time I burnt my wand hand in the cauldron? What if I screwed up somewhere along the line?

We enter the pitch-black grandstands as the three whirling, twirling dragons ignite the torches in a synchronized, single breath. Then it's a series of speeches on rigor, respect, responsibility and a few other r-words that I can't remember. All I can think about is how I won't cry when I stand by the podium and wait for the banners that won't arrive. I might be embarrassed, but I'll still be dignified.

Still, I wonder if maybe my dad is right. I'm a strong reader. I'm great at designing things. Maybe, just maybe, a lower level school might pick me up as a charity case – a token firt to help the students who need help learning how to memorize their spells. Or maybe someone who could tutor kids on the Schnorbitz team. I could be a Spell Checker, underlining any mistakes with a red ink quill.

There haven't been any total rejections since Filbert. Then again, most firts are quietly pulled out of school at a younger age. They spend their days at home reading books and sketching on parchment or sneaking off to Noah's Arcade.

I pick at my nails as the A's stream by, one at a time. Even the dorkiest wizards get a few banners and a polite applause. That could be me.

Just fade away into the background of a discount academy.

My mind wanders through the beginning of the B's. I snap to attention when I hear "Sarah Bellum" from the phonograph. Sarah walks to the stage, head held high while a mob of banners swirl around her, each competing for her attention.

She waves her wand and the banners fall to the floor like crumpled paper bags.

"What's she doing?" Scotty whispers as Sarah picks up each one and folds them like she's doing laundry. She saunters toward the principal and hands her the stack with a calm "no thank you."

"Did you see all of those invitations?" Scotty whispers.

It makes no sense. Sarah's pretty much an orphan and her family is stuck living in a shack at the graveyard. I can't possibly see what would keep her in our village instead of going off to an elite academy. This is her chance to get away.

The audience continues to murmur until they call Bruno Buchanan to the stage. He pretends to be surprised by the sheer number of banners wrapping him up like a mummy. He winks at the audience, feigns interest in each school and finally snags the shimmering gold banner of the Fancy Shmancy Magical Academy for Great and Awesome and Even Occasionally Terrible Wizards.

All twelve letter-C students walk up, choose their banners, bow to the crowd and step down from the platform.

Suddenly, I'm in no hurry to get it over with. I consider my options. I could pretend I need to use the restroom. As I glance at the troll patrolling the seats, I decide against it. Okay, I was wrong. It turns out there aren't too many options.

I know my turn is coming up when Samantha Dowling snags a banner for the Pretty Good Discount School for the Mostly-Magical Kids. She looks disappointed, but not surprised. Maybe they'll hold a slot for me, too. Samantha can't spell a spell to save her life.

"Wendell Darrell Drackenberger," the principal announces. Her words echo through the flowery megaphones floating above us. I walk to the stage. Okay, that's not entirely true. I stumble forward, barely making it to the podium.

I wait for a banner. Nothing happens. I wait again. Still nothing. Maybe someone will usher me away politely. The crowd begins whispering. I turn toward my principal, hoping she'll send me down. She shakes her head.

My heart races. I'm lightheaded under the floating lanterns lighting the stage.

"Can I go?" I mouth out, but no one signals me forward.

"Please?" I plead.

"You may go," my principal says in a barely audible voice. Right as I turn away, a stray banner flips around and falls toward me. The crowd gasps. It has to be a mistake. However, it's there, dancing around, telling me that maybe there's a place for a firt after all.

I turn to the principal. "Um, someone left this, I think."

"Go on," she says.

I step closer to the shimmering gold banner. The crimson words pop off the fabric and float toward my eyes. It's the Fancy Shmancy Magical Academy for Great and Awesome and Even Occasionally Terrible Wizards. I wait. The principal nods.

Could they actually want me? Is it possible that they want to hook me up with a few elves so that I can become a Designer or a Maker? I'm trying to move, but I'm stuck. I can't grab the banner. *Calm down. Take a deep breath.* I reach for the banner, but it twirls around behind me.

"Just grab the banner!" a heckler yells.

"It's because of his family," a woman says to her husband. "You know the Drackenbergers. They get what they want."

"He's a fraud! He's a firt!" a voice echoes through the grandstands.

Just breathe. Take a step. Pull the banner and let it go.

The crowd murmurs again.

"Just take it," my principal whispers. "Go on."

I can't move. The banner is hovering around me, but I can't move. I turn to my principal again.

"Go ahead," she mouths out. The banner hovers around my neck, but I can't move.

Another deep breath. I snatch the banner and hold it up for the audience. Instantly it disintegrates into gold dust, the shimmering pieces falling to the floor. The crowd doesn't laugh. They don't clap. A few murmur. Most of them wait, hoping for the awkward moment to end.

I swallow hard and hold back tears. An illusory charm. One last prank on the way out.

This right here is why Bruno earned a spot at Fancy Shmancy Magical Academy for Great and Awesome and Even Occasionally Terrible Wizards. What's the worst they can do? Expel him from a school he just finished?

"I'm so sorry," my principal says, patting me on the back.

"It's okay," I lie.

However, it's not okay and she knows it. I spend the rest of the ceremony telling myself not to cry. I hold on to that as my only consolation. Bruno never sees me cry.

After they call the last student forward, Dr. Schmorbenpopper taps her wand on the podium. "We have a last minute change of schedule. I need every student who did not receive a banner to exit immediately and head toward the secret hidden room."

I'm not sure why they bother calling it hidden if everyone knows that it's in the back of the lobby. Come to think of it, I don't see why they call it a secret, either.

Mr. Oglesby adjusts his glasses and reads from a parchment, "Could I get all the firts to form a line?"

"It's just me," I mutter.

"I suppose it is just you," he clears his throat. "Mr. Dragonbooger?"

"Drackenberger," I correct him.

"Oh, yes, I suppose it is. I just assumed that because your family is full of great wizards, you had to have a different last name."

"Nope, I'm a member of the Drackenberger family . . . for now."

"That's right. You were the little firt I met earlier today."

He flicks his wand and a chamber opens. I follow him to a tiny stonewall room lit only by a single candle. It smells like mildew and old people. Not that I make it a habit of smelling mildew – or old people for that matter, but you get the point.

"It's so rare that we have a firt. We don't really have much practice with this," he says blowing the dust off a stack of parchments.

"I see."

He hands me a pamphlet called *So, This Is a Little Bit Awkward, But, Yeah, You Don't Have Any Magical Powers.* I'm including the pamphlet in this book. You can take it right there and cut it out. If you want, you can hand it over to someone you know who isn't magical; which, I suppose is just about everyone you know.

SO, THIS IS A LITTLE BIT AWKWARD, BUT, YEAH, YOU **DON'T HAVE ANY** MAGICAL POWERS.

a pamphlet brought to you by the council of counsel

Give up on your hopes of owning a castle. Your jobs are pretty much limited to street sweeper, dragon groomer or cauldron cleaner.

While other kids will be **waving** wands, you will be **waiving** your wand.

You will not earn your broom permit. However, there's always unicycles. Or, if you're feeling brave, try riding a bear.

a pamphlet brought to you by the council of counsel

He twirls his wand and a filthy cupboard pops open, revealing a film projector that he slides to the middle of the table. Waving his wand again., he says, "Okay, let's go. Begin the show."

As the reel clicks and twirls, a grainy black and white projection appears against the wall. The gray figure floats off the wall and steps toward me.

"So, kid, you're feeling like you're not magical? You're feeling like you're not special? You're feeling like you have no future?
Well guess what? You're absolutely right."

I turn to Mr. Oglesby, "Hey, what's that for? I thought this was supposed to make me feel . . ."

"Eyes on me, kid," the gray man snarls.

"Are you a ghost?" I ask.

Mr. Oglesby cuts in, "Nope, it's a new interactive form of motion picture. He's charmed to answer your questions. Pretty nifty, eh?"

"If you're feeling bad about yourself, you should be, because you're just not magical. Maybe if you had paid closer attention in class things might have worked out for you."

"But I tried my hardest," I say.

"Your hardest? Really? You never daydreamed in charms class? You never snuck items from the DUMP?"

I shift in my chair. How does he know about that?

"I really tried," I repeat.

He continues, "You will be staying at home all day from this point on. No more school. Consider yourself lucky. It's like having a ditch day every day of the year."

"Well, I don't want to ditch," I say.

"Then think of it this way. You get to skip school, skip work and go straight into retirement. Do you know that most wizards wish they had the kind of free time that you'll have?"

"What am I supposed to do all day?"

"Even without magic, you can read a book or look at a rock or look at a wall. Or you could look at a different wall. When that gets old, you have two more walls that you can look at. You could look at your chair. And, I don't know if your family keeps plants, but you could look at your plants. Did I mention that you could look at the wall? I highly recommend wall watching."

"Can I go to the DUMP?" I ask in frustration.

"It's disgusting."

I nod.

"Any questions?"

I clear my throat. "So, I won't get to use a broom?"

"Nonsense," he says, "You just can't *ride* one. However, you can use a broom all you want for sweeping. See, there's something else you can do all day. Consider your hours sweeping as practice for being a street sweeper. It's a great field for a firt."

"I'll keep that in mind," I mutter. Suddenly the reality sets in. I won't be magical. Ever. I'll be like the crazy lady that cleans cauldrons at Liz Anya's Italian Eatery.

The motion picture continues, "This is the worst day of your life. However, the good news is this: it won't get any worse than today. It only gets better from here. So, that's a plus."

The projection flickers off. I sit alone with my pamphlet waiting for Mr. Oglesby to let me know when I can leave.

"It'll be soon," he says, pulling out his pocket watch. "We wouldn't want it to be awkward when the others get out. We don't want to ruin it for them."

I wait by the lone candle while Mr. Oglesby paces the corridor. A few trolls pass by complaining that their green room wasn't green enough and their steak was too rare.

Finally, Mr. Oglesby jumps in, waves his wand and waits for the door to lock.

"Wendell, this could be your big opportunity," he whispers.

"I don't understand what you're talking about."

"I know you want to visit the DUMP," he whispers.

"I'm not going to pull a Filbert. I was just . . . I was curious about it."

"Wendell, I've been paying closer attention to you than you think and so what I mention isn't something out of a whim. Bezaudorf needs you."

It's an odd thing to say from someone who can't get my name right. I shake my head. "I don't get what you're saying."

"Of course. I've been pretty opaque. You and I both know that the Misfits are going to attack again. I personally believe that Filbert is still alive. You would be the perfect covert operative."

"I don't even know what a covert operative is," I admit.

"A spy. You could go to the DUMP and find out what's going on with the Misfits. Honestly, I'm surprised they haven't tried to contact you thus far."

I consider telling him about Benny, but instead I shrug my shoulders. I'm in no mood to help our village. Not after tonight. Besides, it's not like I have anything to offer. I'm a firt.

We wait in silence for another half hour before he informs me that I can go. I follow him down the corridor and into the empty grandstands. A few stray banners still twirl back and forth in a game of tag, waiting for the clean-up crew to apply the final charms.

SIX
AN UNEXPECTED INVITATION

I step outside into the blazing colors of magicworks shimmering and taking on new forms above the lake. Head hung low, I trudge across the wobbly bridge and head toward the edge of Restaurant Row (which is actually anything but a row). The phonographs pulse with party tunes while the self-propelling guitars and bewitched banjos struggle to keep up with the pace. It's a barrage of yelling and jumping and cartwheels - and that's just the adults.

I dodge a flock of mobile messages and sidestep the plank of Swashbuckler's Confectionary, where kids are gorging themselves on Whirling Fireballs and Crackling Candy Corn. I push through the crowds at the

Town Tetrahedron and pass the slapdash tree house of Sally's Smart Mart, where the books are opened tonight and the images hover off the pages, reminding the village of past heroic wizards. As I cross the alley of Spell It Correctly!, I notice a picture. Probably just another stray mobile message knocked down in the revelry of Invitation Night.

I reach down to throw it away, but the picture isn't moving. I snag a floating lantern and position it above the photograph. The image remains still. A woman is smiling, holding a toothbrush. Not a charmed one, either. She's clearly doing the work herself, using an elixir that leads to an unnatural color of white. Her shirt has no buttons or ruffles or anything remotely decorative. It looks like it's knit right onto her. Strange.

I look both ways. Trying not to appear suspicious, I tuck it into my tattered robe and walk away coolly. A few paces forward, I notice a second photograph and rush to the hovering lantern so quickly that it hits my head.

I shake off the pain and snatch the picture. This one is even more amazing. A family is taking a machine out for a picnic. I'm not sure what the robot would eat (perhaps oil?) but everyone is smiling. I look closely at the shimmering metal, curved to perfection. Wheels! Smart move. Instead of giving their robot feet, they use wheels. Apparently, the robot's name is Bronco (or maybe he's just a robotic bronco) and his specifications are laid out clearly – how many miles he can run in a gallon, how many horses he can overpower.

This has to be from the DUMP and yet it doesn't seem dirty at all. It seems light. Really light, with colors brighter than anything we have in Bezaudorf.

I slip the inanimate photo into my pocket and continue down the alley. Shadows shift. Steps echo. I jump at a clicking sound. Pausing, I look around. Nothing. Yet as I pick up my stride, the echoing footsteps continue.

My silk shirt is now drenched. I can feel the sweat dripping down my nose, despite the winter air around me. My pulse pounds. I can taste the sweat beading up on my lips. The alley has never felt so empty or so long before. I jog forward, my breath streaming out like a dragon.

"What do you have?" a voice calls out from the shadows. I shake my head.

"Just show me what you have," he says again. I dart down the alley and back into the Town Tetrahedron, knocking down a candy cart on the along the way. As I spin around to see if anyone is following me, a twirling fireball grazes my shoulder and lands on my robe. Jumping up, I shake the flames away and then try my best to blend in.

I snake through the crowd until I see it. Another picture. This one is larger. I survey the street. Nobody sees the treasure. To my right I notice more. The bobbing lantern gives just enough light to catch the bold red letters. *Mediocre Home and Gardens.* It's not just a picture, but an entire booklet filled with words and pictures of the DUMP.

I seize the booklet and roll it up like a baton. A light flashes. I run. Not a jog, either. No, I sprint past the brooms parked outside of Baldwin's Pure Bread Bakery. Out of nowhere, I trip and skid along the cobblestone streets.

A hideous-looking troll hovers over me.

"Did you enjoy your trip?"

I shake my head.

"Can I guess your favorite season? Would it happen to be *fall*?"

He offers a hand, but I shake my head. Towering over me (well, as best as he can given his height), he points his finger in my face. "What? You think you're too good to touch a troll? You of all wizards. The firt is too good to get a helping hand from a troll."

"Y-Y-You just tripped me," I stammer.

"Argh!" he growls.

"Look, I'm sorry. I didn't mean to offend you, I swear. Just let me go home, okay? I've got a party to go to."

"Spechwalph," a familiar voice calls out. "Leave the boy alone." It's Benny and he's running as fast as his little legs can carry him.

"Benny, this troll was trying to . . ."

He shakes his head and pulls me up. "I told him to stop you. I didn't realize he would trip you. Follow me."

I trail behind, unsure of whether I should walk or jog. Meanwhile, he's attempting a near-sprint toward the Gnome Home (a modest, mostly underground mound at the edge of the Town Tetrahedron).

"He's pretty rude," I point out.

"Well, he's the Employee of the Month. Then again, I only have three employees and they're all trolls."

I duck down as we step toward the counter. I might be the shortest thirteen-year-old in Bezaudorf, but I'm a giant among gnomes.

Spechwalph steps in.

The waiter, Gnome Chomsky, glares at him. "We don't serve trolls."

"Well, that's a good thing, because I'm not in the habit of eating trolls. Now gimme a bacon-wrapped cupcake."

Gnome Chomsky nods and points to me. "What'll you have to drink?"

"I'll have a hot chocolate," I answer, still shivering from the December air.

"We don't have hot chocolate. Would you like a hot gravy instead?"

"I'll pass," I answer.

"And you?" he turns to Benny.

"I'll pass . . . a ton of gas when I'm done with a piping hot mug of gravy."

He hands Benny his mug and passes me a cup of hot butterscotch with marshmallows. "It's not on the menu," he whispers. "However, I figured you could use it tonight. I heard about the ceremony."

"Check out my office," Benny says, heading to a backroom. He waves his wand and instantly the lanterns flame up.

The room is packed full of devices that beep and buzz and whistle. It's a mix of tubing and touch-screens and vials of glowing liquids. On the far end, he has a map lit, not by a candle, but a white ball that lets out the steadiest stream of light I've ever seen. Above it, the words, "MISFIT ATTACK PLANS" scream out in bold letters.

This has to be the Misfit lair. I take a deep breath and step inside.

"Wow," is all I can manage to say.

"It's not exactly landscaping, now, is it?" he grins.

"Not so much."

"This is very cool," I admit.

"Fairy cool? Is that what you think? Do you see wings? I'm a gnome, Wendell. Not a fairy. I've lived across the street from you for how long?"

I shake my head. "No, I mean very cool."

"I suppose it is," he says, waving his wand and adding a quick heating charm. "Now, let's talk about business. You could work with me. You'd be my apprentice. I could use a designer."

I shake my head. "I . . . um . . . I don't know." The bright Misfits logo flashes through my mind.

He walks over and grabs a pair of glasses and a tiny box with loops of wires.

"Listen, I could use your help. See, I have this project of sorts. It has to do with not only Bezaudorf but the entire enchanted world," his eyes light up. Literally. His glasses have a special light sensor on them and now he has creepy lit-up eyes.

"I don't think so," I mumble.

"They mocked you. Didn't give you any points for your mind, now did they?"

"I'm a firt," I confess.

"You have magic that they overlooked, because it didn't look the way they wanted it to look. You're a Maker, Wendell. A Designer. I believe that you deserve a chance," he says.

"Thanks, but . . ."

He waves his hand and continues, "Now, see, next Saturday is different. Next Saturday we will have our revenge. They'll see our powers. You'll prove yourself to be the ultimate engineer," he says, stepping up on a stool and patting my shoulder.

"Let me think about it."

He scratches his beard and continues. "I'll prove that I'm just as good as the elves and you'll get your revenge on the village."

"I don't know," I whisper. "Isn't that when kids will be going to their new schools?"

"It's a perfect day for the Misfits," he says with a grin. "Your obnoxious brother will be up there with that bully kid, Bruno. They'll be all smug in their carriage."

"I don't know." His offer is tempting.

"I need your help. Admit it. You want to get back at them after tonight. You would work with the DUMP and see things other wizards don't get to see. You're already the exception. Isn't it time you became exceptional?"

SEVEN
THE UNSURPRISED PARTY

I approach our castle door and knock.

"Shh . . ." someone says.

A few hushed voices whisper counter-candle curses. I knock again.

The door bursts open with a deafening, "Surprise!"

"Um, yeah, about that . . . you told me there was going to be a party this afternoon. So it's not really a surprise," I point out.

My mom winces. "Okay, go on then. Step back and we'll do this the right way."

I knock again. She opens the door and everyone screams. "Not surprised at all!"

A banner floats above the fireplace reading, "Hey Wendell, Congratulations on being magical."

I point to the sign. "Mom, I'm not magical. You were there. I was officially classified as a firt."

"Good point," she mutters. With a quick wave of her wand, the banner reads, "Hey Wendell, congratulations on not being magical." She turns her head up, thinks for a moment and adds, " . . . yet" to the end.

"Maybe we should call off the party," my dad suggests. "Let the boy go to his room and be alone. It was a pretty rough day for him."

"But we have cake," my mom says.

"But he isn't magical," Greg points out.

"We have cake," my mom argues.

"But the boy isn't special," my uncle cuts in.

"Cake is special," my mom says

"But there's nothing to celebrate," my uncle argues.

My mom stands on a chair and speaks above the crowd. "Well, we have cake and cake is reason enough to celebrate. Who doesn't like cake?" She turns to the small crowd. "Does anyone here not like cake?"

Not a hand in the air.

"See. Now, who likes cake?" Every hand shoots up in unison.

"I like cake," my sister yells.

"Me, too," my brown-nosing brother adds.

"Hooray for cake!" my grandma yells. Then turning to me, she asks, "Now, why are we eating cake again?"

"Because I'm not magical," I point out.

"Sure you are. You're more magical than that bratty brother of yours in that fancy dandy dippy do school for great wizards," she says. Smiling she adds, "You're magical. You just don't know it. Magic is all around if you're paying attention."

My mom takes the cake out from the box, but my dad doesn't let up. "See this right here. This is why I told you not to plan a party for him. I wanted to take him out of school altogether. I told you he wasn't magical. You can't just make things true by hoping that they're true. He's a firt. Always has been. The sooner you get used to that idea, the easier it will be for him."

In most castles, this would lead to awkward silence. Not in our family. Nobody notices. They're all too busy cutting cake and busting out the enchanted candy to notice my dad's words. My grandma sucks on a Fire Ball and nearly lights Greg on fire when she belches out a stream of flames.

He stares at her as he wipes the ashes off his fancy dress robes.

"I forgot they weren't peppermint," she smiles (conveniently "forgetting" she doesn't have her dentures in, either).

Minutes later, Benny stops by. "I got you a present. I figured it would help you out with the boredom."

"What are you doing here?" I ask.

"Please, Wendell. Be polite. He brought you a gift."

I plow through the Merry Christmas wrapping paper and stare at the box. Bored Games – a dull new game for wizards who live boring lives.

"Oh, that's lovely," my mom says with her mouth full of cake.

"Designed it myself back when I worked for the elves," Benny says. "Of course I never really understood the need for boring games. But when they said, 'Just design a bored game,' I did exactly that."

"Um, yeah, thanks," I mutter.

"It never sold too well," he says, scooping out cake with his bare hand.

"I can't imagine why," I respond.

"You know, you could always join me as an apprentice," he says.

"Oh, that would be great," my dad says. "You could learn all about the art of lawn maintenance. It's a dignified job for a firt."

My mind races back to the room at the Gnome Home. It's tempting. Instead of playing Bored Games all day, I could design a robot. Then again, it sounds like he's planning something for the Misfits. I want to design things. I just don't want them to be used to terrorize the village.

Soon the party rolls into the enchanted piñata stage (with the crackling candy corn burning holes in our couches). I grab a handful of chocolate-covered pumpkin seeds and slip away to my bedroom while the family continues to have their party – not in honor of me, but in honor of cake.

They forget to use a heating charm, so the room is freezing. However, when Ash cuddles up next to me, I no longer shiver. As I pull off my robe, I notice the thin, colorful book.

I flip through the pages. They have elixirs that keep your face free of wrinkles. They eat chocolate-covered doves and put a mayonnaise-like miracle whipped topping on their sandwiches. Maybe they're not all that different from us.

Don't get me wrong. There was a time when the disenchanted hated us. Medieval scribes used fairy blood for glitter pens. Ignorant villagers burned witches at the stake. Now we realize that the DUMP isn't dangerous, so much as dirty. However, I'm starting to think that they're wrong about that. With each picture I examine, the DUMP feels more enchanted.

I could go there. I mean, being non-magical and all, I could blend right in. If it turns out to be truly dirty, I could run back into our world.

I'm definitely going tomorrow.

Or maybe not. I mean, my parents would be angry if they knew about my plans to visit the DUMP. My mom calls the DUMP "crummy," which is about as nasty a word as she'll ever say. She points to Filbert as evidence that the DUMP attracts the worst riffraff around.

As I flip through the pages again, the door pops open. I toss the booklet under the blanket and sigh. I'm going.

My dad startles me with an awkward wave. I fall off my bed and slip the DUMP book into my robe.

"Hey, Wendell, how are you doing?"

"Do I have to answer?"

"That bad?" he asks.

REASONS TO BELIEVE THAT THEY LOVE US

Witches and wizards are now heroes in the disenchanted people's books. Then again, so are 120-year-old creepy voyeuristic vampires.

We're also heroes in their motion pictures.

They aren't burning witches at the stake anymore. So, that's a real plus.

REASONS TO BELIEVE THAT THEY HATE US

They named their worst basketball team after us.

People boycott us.

On Halloween, kids dress up like us and threaten to vandalize people ("tricks") if they don't get candy.

"Well, I'm an embarrassment to the whole family."

"That's not true. Not true at all. See, I learned a long time ago not to expected anything of you and you know what? I wasn't disappointed as a result. Tonight didn't surprise me one bit."

"Oh," is all I can manage.

"Yeah, I'll love you no matter what – even if you don't amount to anything."

I think that's supposed to make me feel better, but it doesn't work. I need to see myself beyond my magical shortcomings. I want to amount to something, even if it's not magical. As he starts telling me the Tale of the Stinky Flower (available on the next page), I quit listening.

All I can think about is going to the DUMP tomorrow.

THE NINJAS AND THE STINKY FLOWER

ILLUSTRATED BY WENDELL DRACKENBERGER

Once upon a time, there was a girl named Patricia, who couldn't smell anything.

She often brought back strange toys, like rotten fish.

One day, she found a beautiful flower.

Unbeknownst (really, who uses that term?) to her, the flower was stinky. A mere sniff of the flower could induce vomit.

Her mother placed the flower in a vase, but secretly wished that it would die.

One day, a group of angry ninjas attacked her house. Her family was defenseless.

But the stench of the flower caused the ninjas to throw up and then leave.

EIGHT
A QUEST TO THE D.U.M.P.

I wake up the next morning and fumble through my slightly charred blanket. Next time, I'm grabbing the fireproof dragon fur blanket from Greg's room.

I reach for the *Mediocre Home and Garden* booklet, but it's gone.

"Ash Lee?" I mumble.

The old dragon stretches her legs and nudges her snout against my face.

"Ash?"

She turns around and coughs. Flaky ashes everywhere. I shake my head. Maybe the booklet isn't completely destroyed. But as she belches out a flame, I catch a flittering picture of a silver box.

I clench my fists, but she drops her ears and lowers her head. "It's okay, girl. You just need a new chew toy, don't you?"

She wags her tail, whipping the door open in anticipation. Wizards claim that dragons can't understand language, but I swear she knows the word "toy."

I follow her out to the family room.

"She needs a wingcut, Wendell," my dad yells from the observatory.

This is it. It has to be today. Otherwise I'll chicken out. I dart down to the kitchen and pull out five quills before I can find a single one with working ink. I write a note explaining that I will be heading to the library.

Stepping out into the frosty air, I stare at Benny's well-manicured lawn. I still can't make sense out of Benny and the Misfits. If Benny is really behind the attacks, I don't want to help him. I mean, yeah, I'm angry. Last night was humiliating. However, I don't want revenge.

Then again, if I don't help him, he might get angry and if he's really angry, he might make our castle his first target. My mind flashes back to last night. It would be fun to work with machines. Wrong, but fun.

"No," I mumble to myself. "I couldn't live with myself if I did. Maybe I'll just explain to him that I'm not interested but that I'll leave him alone and I won't tell anyone anything.

I dash across the road and knock on his small door. Nobody answers. Maybe he's buying an overpriced coffee from Tar Shucks (where the coffee is as thick as tar). More like a hot gravy at the Gnome Home.

"Benny? You there?" Nobody answers.

I pound this time. "You home?" As I step away, a paper flaps nervously around me. I snatch it. The mobile message reads:

```
This   morning   is   just   the
beginning. We  need  to  plan  for
next Saturday.
```

I slip the note in my back pocket and meander around the hut.

"Hello? Benny?" Nobody answers. I slip around the back and look for the crooked pot. It's been replaced by a new pot in the perfect row lining his back patio. As I round the corner again, I notice another note slipping down and sliding under the door. I jump forward and catch it with the edge of my boot.

The pathetic paper flaps around, straining to make it through the door. However, it's no match for my boot. Holding my foot down, I trap the note and snag it before it can slip away.

```
Benny,
   Don't feel too bad. We did
   what we could and we
   accomplished a lot.
   Think of today as more of a
   Practice run for the
   real battle.
                    - F.P.
```

I slip the note into my back pocket and head down the road. It still doesn't make sense. Benny was the hero who stopped the Misfits. Why would he be working for them now?

The keeper at Gwynn's Galloping Unicorn Utopia hardly bothers with a wave. "You can shovel unicorn manure if you can't find a job," he says with a haggard expression.

"Thanks," I holler back as I head down the cobblestone. The charms are all worn out as I pass Noah's arcade and head into the Town Tetrahedron. A few stray accordions wheeze out their fading magical tunes while the once-lively banners now limp around at eye-level. It's as if the whole village just had Christmas and nobody wants to deal with the wrapping paper.

A sleep-flying fairy twirls around my face. "Excuse me, ma'am."

The purple-winged creature spins around, fists clenched. "Who ya calling ma'am?"

"Sorry. Sorry. I didn't mean to . . ."

"You see this mustache?" he says, pointing to his thread-sized facial hair.

"I'm sorry," I respond.

"Yeah, well I got more magic in this tiny pinky than you'll ever have, ya firt."

"I'm sorry. You are definitely a male fairy. I made a bad assumption based on your purple wings."

"You know, for centuries purple was the color of royalty. I'm very dig . . ." he lets out a belch seven times his size. "I'm *the* Dignified Dr. Larry Faerie the Fairy."

"I understand," I say, trying to out-walk his crooked flying. Suddenly it hits me. "Why aren't you with the fairies? I mean, aren't you supposed to be nocturnal?"

Without so much as a goodbye, he zips past me and flies toward the forest. As I enter the Town Tetrahedron a commotion stirs. The lethargic feel is replaced with a sudden buzz. What's going on? Why is a crowd forming on the opposite end?

"Did you hear about what happened?" a woman asks.

"I don't think it was a dragon. If you ask me, I think Filbert's back. I don't think he ever died."

"That's what happens when you're not magical. You start going rogue. Just watch what happens with the dragon booger kid."

I approach Sweet Treat Tweet Street (the avenue for birds and bakeries). Say that seven times fast. No, really, set this book down and try it. I told you it was hard to do.

Suddenly, the commotion makes sense. The smell of toasted marshmallows wafts through the air. The road is slick with crystallized sugar. I can hear the crackling flames licking the slapdash structure of Flour Power.

Wait a second. Quick Quest Cartographers is just behind it. I shake my head. It can't be. Is Benny already retaliating against my family?

"Mom!" I yell.

It's a sea of black, with smoke-covered wizards pushing their way out of the street.

"Please clear out of the way," the phonographs boom. The crowd ignores the instructions as eight witches, led by the Head Alchemist train their wands at a fire. Clouds form above the smoke. Pushing through the throngs of wizards, I hear the screaming. A boy at Flour Power is holding his bloody leg.

"The apothecary's full," a man says, guiding a hovering stretcher.

"That's my son!" a woman yells. "Make another storey. You've got the incantations to do it."

I have to find my mom. She's probably stuck inside the building denying that anything bad even happened. I slip on the street, still slick with burnt sugar. The cloud above me grows larger.

Crash. What starts as a drizzle grows into a downpour. Pulse pounding, I push through the crowd. I can't see past the massive mast at Swashbuckler's Confectionary.

An invisible force pushes back as I rush toward the deck.

"This area is off limits," an officer says, tipping his enchanted hat.

"But my mom works at Quick Quest Cartographers. I need to see if she's okay."

"I can't let you through," he says, shrugging his shoulders.

"Can I just find out if she's okay?"

He shakes his head. A flock of mobile messages swirl around, fighting against the downpour. "As you can see, communication is limited."

"Can you tell me if Quick Quest was attacked?"

He shakes his head. "I need you to leave," he says reaching for his camera. With a flash of light and a puff of smoke, an image floats away. I step forward and study it.

"Hey, that's confidential!" he yells, reaching for his wand. It's too late. I see it. The front side of Clark's Cobbler is crushed, but everything on Dusty Rhode Rode Road is still pristine. I breathe a sigh of relief at the intact fancy façade of my mom's workplace.

I head toward Mildred's Magical Snow Cones still in a daze. The cacophony of screams grows distant as I take a detour to the Sedentary Cemetery ("where death is always a grave matter") and try to clear my lungs.

"Hey, Mildred, can I get a peppermint snow cone?"

"You sound shaken," she says.

"I just need a snow cone," I tell her. I know, it makes no sense in the dead of winter, but I need something – anything – that will feel normal.

"I can read your mind, Wendell. You'd like a snow cone," she grins.

"Yeah, but I already said that."

MILDRED'S PREDICTIONS

Mildred lost her fortune-teller's license and the only way to gain it back is by having a near-perfect accuracy rate. So, here's how she does it.

"YOU WILL DIE."

The key here is in not naming a specific date. Everyone dies. Life has a 100% mortality rate. So, she wins on this one every time.

"YOU WILL YAWN IN THE NEXT MINUTE."

This one is tricky. She says the prophecy and then yawns. Afterward, it becomes contagious. In fact, you're probably going to yawn right now.

"YOU WILL BUY A NEW HAT."

Enchanted hats wear out. Either the material fails or the charms begin to fade.

"True. But now you're thinking that I can't read your mind," she says. "Well . . . that's what you're thinking, isn't it?"

I shake my head. "I guess that's true, but . . ."

"Now you're thinking 'I just want my snow cone.' That's what you were thinking, right?"

"I guess, but . . ."

"And now you're thinking I'm a phony and that you prefer me as a snow cone maker and not a fortune-teller."

"That's true, but . . ."

She shoots her snow cone cannon straight up in the air and collects each sliver of falling ice.

She looks into my eyes. "That's not why you're here, though. You want to know about the DUMP."

"How'd you . . ."

"I can read your mind, Wendell." She leans in. "I do have the gift of prophecy."

"You smell like smoke," I point out.

"I was at Baldwin's Pure Bread Bakery and next thing I knew the whole street was up in flames. I mean, I guess that's what they get for decorating with cotton candy and marshmallow cream without using any anti-flame spells." She shakes her head.

"Are the Misfits back?"

She nods.

"Is Filbert alive?"

"I doubt it. I'm not pointing any fingers, but I think it's Benny. I never saw him as a hero."

"You think so?"

She hands me my snow cone. "I think he was working with Filbert the whole time and Filbert faked his death."

I shrug. "The other day you mentioned having me join you as a smuggler."

She waves her finger at me. "You don't want to do that. Not today."

"But you just asked me two days ago if I wanted to join you . . ."

"Listen, you can't go. Guards are all over the catacombs, especially after this morning. They'll be sending the zombies out on patrol. Lots of zombies. Trust me. Stay away." She sighs. "Just let this blow over and I'll show you next week."

She has a point. However, I know that if I wait until next week, I'll be too afraid.

"I want to go today."

"It's not going to happen, Wendell. Did you see the damage? Do you really want to be caught?"

"But it's not illegal to go to the DUMP," I point out.

"True, but they're looking for suspects fleeing the village. You fit the profile of a Misfit."

"I'll be careful. I promise."

She pulls off her glasses and rubs her eyes. "Better I tell you than have you go on your own and get devoured by the zombies. Okay, if you really want to see the DUMP, you have to go through the catacombs," she points to the edge of the graveyard. "The key is to keep going straight. Don't take any turns. You can miss the zombies if you time it right. Leave at precisely eight o'clock. You have to go at exactly the pace of 'Twinkle Twinkle Little Star.' No faster, no slower."

I turn away with my snow cone. She taps me on the shoulder, "Oh, and one more thing, a prophecy for free, just because you're such a great customer. You will meet a kid named Phil and together you will build a great Row Dot that will save our village."

"What does that mean?"

"Beats me," she says. "The prophecy is a little fuzzy at this point. The reception might be bad. However, this much is clear: Phil has a Mohawk. You might have to initiate conversation, but you're destined to know him."

I pace around the Sedentary Cemetery, clutching my satchel and pretending to be visiting the departed.

Sarah's house isn't far away, but her parents are ghosts and don't take kindly to the living stopping by unannounced.

I read headstones and check my pocket watch. Still, the minutes crawl by from 7:40 to 8:00.

Finally, I approach the entrance of the unmarked catacomb. It's dark. Really dark. A simple light spell would make a huge difference right now. However, I'm a firt, so that's not going to happen.

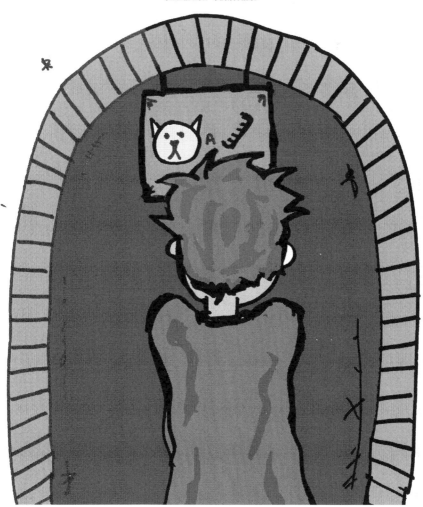

I step inside. *Twinkle. Twinkle.* My steps echo. I breathe in and choke on the musty smell. *Little star.* More steps. I force my legs to move. I jump at the squeaky rats scurrying past. Something wraps around my face. I can't see anything. I wipe away my face and spit it out. Ah, the familiar feel of spider webs.

Just settle down. What was I on? *How I wonder.* Am I going too slowly? Too fast? Is it one step per word? Or is it more of a dance? I don't dance.

My legs wobble. Another step. *Just breathe. Sing the song and go.*

I continue humming, finding a stride, marching into the inky black. More steps. I repeat the song twice. Shouldn't I be at the end by now?

I jump again at a howling ghoul. The garbled laughter echoes through the chambers.

A light appears. Shadows dance. To my left, I notice a shelf of mummified bodies. The scent of fresh herbs permeate the musty catacombs. A fresh body.

I push forward right as the light grows brighter. I stop as a zombie paces forward, the torchlight illuminating his sagging skin. A heavy, rotten odor permeates the air.

He turns back and stares as I continue stepping forward. Nothing. I breathe out. Wait, where am I in the song? Did I skip a line? Is this too fast?

Shadows bounce as the chamber opens into a maze of corridors. Keep straight. Keep moving. The pace is right. The words are gone, but I'm humming it still.

The muttering zombies call out in their guttural tongue. I continue. A zombie turns the corner, brushing against my robe as I walk. Three more paces and another walks past, the flame singeing my hat.

The light fades and I'm back into the pitch-black. The zombie voices fade away, replaced by a loud leaky pipe above me. Two torches flame up as I stagger forward. The dancing flame illuminates just enough of a dark cavern to give me second thoughts. I step onto a wobbly bridge, swaying with every step.

I slip on a plank. The bridge flips around. Suddenly I'm sideways staring into the dark. I can hear the water rushing below. I climb back over as the bridge flips back.

All at once, it plunges down. My stomach drops. Plummeting down, I brace for the rushing water. I slip further, bouncing down each plank.

It stops. I land on my stomach and wipe at my face. Wait a minute. There's no water. None at all. The sound continues, louder this time. I pause to listen, but my skin is crawling with the slithering snakes wrapping around my body. I pick myself up and crawl toward a dim light. I continue gliding through a rusty metal tube, hoping the snakes are behind me.

The light grows brighter until I reach . . . a plant? Can this really be the end of the catacombs?

I push through the shrubbery and climb forward. Instantly I'm in a grassy field, surrounded by a majestic mist. I turn back, but all I see is a wall of dirt and a braided metal fence.

Taking a deep breath, I step forward. Glistening self-propelled carriages dart down a road, apparently guided by red, yellow and green floating lanterns. Across the street, a crimson-colored enchanted bulls-eye floats above the building. I can't imagine what it's used for. Perhaps giants doing target practice?

Across the docked carriages, there's a brightly-colored, luminescent, floating sign welcoming the some kind of queen of dairy and another for the king of burgers. Yep, pretty majestic. Even their food has royalty.

NINE
BUILD A BOT

The DUMP isn't dirty at all. On the contrary, it's beautiful and exciting and . . . more enchanted than anything in Bezaudorf. It's an explosion of colors that I've never seen, all breaking through a mystical mist.

I step onto the sand (strange so far from a beach) and discover an enclosure with bright swirling tubes connecting to a bridge with shiny pipes. It seems to be built for smaller creatures. Is it a home of some sort? Do elves live among the disenchanted?

I stop to examine a curved pillar with a large bowl – a cauldron of some type? I press a shiny button on the side and wait for fire to appear. Nothing happens. I look down again and push the button. Water drenches my face. I press it again and the water returns. No wand. No spells. Just a button and it works. It's cold outside, but I press the water box again and cup it with my hands. Yep, it's normal water.

I step onto the grass, staring at the carriages whizzing by. They have to be going at least twice as fast as a broom and they look three times more comfortable.

Someone taps my shoulder. I spin around and see a boy with a Mohawk, just as Mildred had described.

"Nice dress," he says.

"Oh, it's not a dress. It's a robe," I point out.

"Wait . . . are you pretending to be a wizard?"

"No, I'm not pretending. I'm a real wizard."

I gasp the moment I say it. I just broke the first rule of visiting the DUMP.

"Then do magic," he says.

"Well, technically, I can't *do* anything magical. But I'm still a wizard."

"Sure you are," he winks.

"No, really, I am. But I'm a firt, which is a non-magical wizard. That's why I'm . . ."

"Well, just a heads up. Wearing a dress around here can get you beat up. Not that I care. I mean, wear what you want. Call it a kilt or a poncho or something. I won't judge you."

"Yeah," is all I can manage, having never heard of a poncho or a kilt.

WHICH IS BETTER?

Enchanted Devices

Devices in the DUMP

"Have you seen a tall guy with black hair?"

I shake my head. "It's my first time here. Who are you looking for?"

"It's just my dad. He didn't show up . . . again." He pulls out an enchanted box.

"Woah! What kind of magic is that?"

"You can check it out if you want," he says handing me the device. "It's a couple years old, though."

"I think it's perfect."

"You don't have a phone?" he asks.

I shake my head and hand him the box. He presses the buttons and scowls. "He's not answering."

"Well, why are you meeting him here if you don't like playing stupid games?"

"It's his thing, I guess. If I had it my way, we'd be building stuff."

"You like designing things?" I ask.

He cocks his head. "Why? Do you like designing things?"

"Yeah. I know it's an elf thing, but I like it."

He stares at me and shakes his head. "You're, um, interesting."

"Thanks."

"Want to see my robotics project?"

I nod eagerly and follow him down a trail made of perfectly symmetrical cement. Apparently, it's called a "sidewalk," even though everyone seems to walk upright.

"It's that way," he points. I begin to cross the street, but he pulls me back.

"You have to use the crosswalk," he says, pointing to a black box in the distance. A group of kids dart across the street, but we walk the extra distance and wait for a mechanical voice to tell us to walk.

"Amazing," I mutter as I marvel at the magic. The robot figured out that we needed to go. It took nothing more than the push of a button.

I try my best to listen as he tells me every detail about himself. His name is Phil, but his family calls him Junior and his parents are divorced and he's really into robots and he hates when his mom makes him eat the pizza crust and he thinks bubble wrap is the greatest thing ever invented.

"I've never seen bubble wrap," I admit.

"Well, you know how people say 'This is the best thing since sliced bread?' It should be 'The best thing since bubble wrap.' Never before has the world fused together form and functionality and fun as it did the day that bubble wrap was invented."

I try to pay attention, but I keep getting distracted by the self-propelling carriages (including one that blares music so loud it makes my stomach rumble – must have a phonograph inside of it). "This village is amazing," I mumble as we head toward the rows of identical houses.

They're not just identical, but perfectly straight. There's nothing remotely slapdash about them. The lawns are immaculate, with evenly cut grass in front of each home. I wonder if Benny has seen these yards.

"You're not from around here, are you?" he raises an eyebrow.

I shake my head. "I'm from an enchanted village called Bezaudorf."

"Riiiight . . ." he says with a wink.

"Where is this place?"

"You mean this city?" he asks.

"Yeah."

"Fresno."

"Ooh, Freeessssnnooo. It even sounds majestic," I respond. Phil pauses to chuckle, but instead he shakes his head.

"And the mystical mist?"

"That's the fog. It's like this all winter. It gets depressing, actually."

As we reach his house, he pulls out a tiny key and presses a button. A massive mechanical door slides open without any hint of a spell. Reading my face, he smiles. "It's just a garage door."

"It's perfect."

I follow him through his house and over to his bedroom, where he shows me the robot parts. "I'm entering a robotics contest. The first round is on Wednesday."

He points to a shelf on the wall. "I'm hoping to add a trophy to my trophy case."

I step over the piles of laundry and study the near-empty shelf. A small blue ribbon hangs, reading, "Participant in the Summer Youth Croquet League." It's deathly still, with no hovering charm whatsoever.

"Well, at least you got a blue ribbon. That's first place, right?"

"Um . . . yeah, first place," he mumbles. "I'm pretty good at croquet."

I step over tiny, brightly colored bricks and make my way over to his desk.

"It will move easier if you do this," I point out, slipping a coupling onto the robotic arm. So it begins. For the rest of the morning, I get lost in the robot design. This world may be foreign, but I am at home the moment I'm connecting gears and wheels and casters. I'm offering ideas on what to do with hubs and chassis and talking about forces and physics. For the first time ever, someone cares what I think about where things should go and what they should do.

A few hours later, he notices that I'm doing the pee pee dance.

"You okay?" he asks.

"I kind-of need to . . ."

"The restroom is down the hall," he points out.

I head toward a room with a bed and a small couch. Yep, this has to be the restroom.

"Um, there's no toilet in here."

He shakes his head. "Across from the living room."

"You have a room for the living? Please tell me you don't have a dead room, too."

"We don't have any dead people," his little sister says.

"Yes we do. Grandpa's ashes are in the living room," Phil says, pointing to an urn. "And yet, we still call it the living room."

I walk past the liveliest room in the house. "That's not the living room. That's the family room," she argues.

"Can I still cross through it if I'm not part of your family?"

They both laugh, so I assume it's safe to cross. I walk past their pictures. There's a picture of Phil with his dad. I have this nagging sense that I've seen him before, maybe on a poster or a newspaper.

"Your dad's not a wizard, is he?" I ask.

"Pretty sure he's not, seeing as how wizards aren't real."

"I feel like I've seen him before," I say, making my way to the bathroom.

I walk back through the hallway and stare at the picture again. I know I've seen that face. I shake my head and head back to his room, where we both work on the robot. I get lost in the project, refusing to get up when he offers a snack.

"I can't believe we're making a robot," I point out. It's both more fantastical and more real than I had imagined. We continue to assemble and disassemble parts, getting lost in our ideas.

He explains the basics of electrical currents and I teach him how he can make the design more flexible and efficient. For the first time ever, I'm building things that move with the push of a button. "It feels like magic," I say.

"It's better than magic. It's engineering," he says. "You don't have to be a wizard to make it work."

"So you really don't have any charms in this place, do you?"

He shakes his head.

"Like the temperature here. That's not a heat charm?"

"That's a heater. And a pretty old one at that," he says. Then he launches into a long explanation of heat and coils. I believe him. It's logical, but on another level, it's still too hard to accept. It feels like a whole world tailored to a guy like me.

Suddenly I notice the setting sun. "Hey, I need to get back to my castle. My mom may not notice, but I guarantee that my dragon will make a fuss if I'm late."

"Right," he winks. "Because you're 'a wizard.' You have to get back to your world."

"It's not really a world, though. It's just a closed-off part of the same earth, like a wrinkle."

"Right," he nods. "Well, because this non-wizard world is new to you, do you want to bring something back?"

He hands me a pencil (which is like a quill, but erasable) and a copy of *Populist Mechanics* (a book about engineering and sticking it to "the Man," whoever that is).

"Hey, about that robotics contest on Wednesday. I could use your help tomorrow. Want to come back?"

"Sure," I say, but I'm not so sure I want to lie to my parents again only to go through zombie-guarded catacombs again.

I sprint past the neighborhood with the identical houses and into the grass with the colorful tubes in the sand, into the catacombs, up the wobbly bridge, past the stench of the zombies and out along the Sedentary Cemetery. I continue sprinting past Mr. Macnology's Site for Sight (where it's always a spectacle of spectacles) and down the cobblestone road toward our castle. I arrive at my castle out of breath.

Melissa meets me at the door. "Wanna practice schnorbitz with me?" she asks, grabbing a new disk from Scott's Sports Shop.

"I'm too tired," I say, stepping into the castle and walking past the scent of pumpkin soup bubbling in the cauldron.

"You're tired from being at the library?" she asks.

"We'll play tomorrow," I say as I march up the stairs.

I'm left with this lingering feeling that maybe the whole "dirty DUMP" thing is just a lie they tell us to keep us wearing robes and hanging around cauldrons when we could be driving cars and using phones.

Then again, maybe the DUMP isn't better so much as different. What if it's perfectly designed for a firt? Have I found where I truly belong? What would it take for me to stay there forever? Ash paws at my robes. Okay, maybe not forever.

I open my desk and pull out the brochure for the Misfits. I re-read the list of values. Without thinking, I nod my head in agreement. The village was awful. Nobody stood by me last night. Then this morning they accused me of joining the Misfits without having any kind of proof.

A disturbing thought flashes through my mind. What if they're right? I've lied to my family and spent the day in the DUMP.

Isn't this how it started with Filbert the Firt? Maybe I'm going rogue. I can imagine the headlines:

An hour later, I'm sitting at the dinner table. My dad brings up the attacks, but my mom quickly chides him for being unpleasant.

"Everything's fine," she says. "It wasn't anywhere near our store."

"It wasn't this time," Greg says. "But it might be next time."

"Are the Misfits back?" Melissa asks.

"Where'd you hear about he Misfits?" my dad asks.

Before she can answer, my mom says, "The Misfits were a long time ago. They're gone. We're safe, sweetheart."

That's the end of it. Nobody dares to break the silence. I leave the dinner before dessert and dart up the stairs. For the rest of the night, I sketch out robot designs. I make lists and more lists and lists of my lists, each time marveling at the fact that I never have to dip a quill or pull out Benny's smelly markers.

When I eventually doze off, I dream of the Misfits. They've got robots. Huge robots. Giant machines hurling fireballs at the village. In the midst of the tears and the chaos and the smoke, I see Greg. His eyes are shut. Lifeless.

I jump out of bed, startling Ash. She stomps behind me as I tiptoe into Greg's room. I have to tell him about the Misfits. However, as I watch him huddle under a blanket, I turn away. I can talk to him in the morning.

TEN
WEIRD WIRED ROBOTICS

I jump out of bed the moment I realize that the sun is already streaming through my window. Greg meets me in the kitchen. I want to tell him about everything about the Misfit attacks planned for Saturday, but it has to be close to eight already. I can talk to him tonight.

"So, how was the library?" he asks.

"It was fine. It was good," I mutter.

"Interesting. You say it was good and fine. I'm not sure there's a difference between the two. But hey, you were there at the library all day, right?"

I nod.

He jumps up and points his oatmeal-soaked spoon at my throat, forgetting that he isn't holding a wand. "You lie. You can't do magic and you lie. What is this family coming to?"

"I'm not lying," I lie.

"Then tell me how you spent all day in the library when it was closed."

I gasp. How can that be? It's always open on Saturdays.

"That's right, Wendell, all of Cole D. Sachs Cul-De-Sac was closed. They found a note threatening the police station. You would have known that if you weren't sneaking out into the DUMP."

I shake my head. "I wasn't at the DUMP. I was . . . I was seeing a girl. And I was . . . um . . . embarrassed to tell you about it."

He shakes his head. "No girl is interested in you, Wendell. You're a firt. You were at the DUMP, weren't you?"

"I wasn't," I lie.

"I saw the yellow drawing stick you left in your room," he says, pulling out the pencil.

"Please don't tell mom or dad," I whisper.

"Are you working for Filbert?"

"No. I mean, of course not. Filbtert's dead," I point out.

"He didn't die. He disappeared. Nobody saw his body and I don't trust Benny's word. I think he's a Misfit, too. And I think he's sending you out to the DUMP to steal more supplies. I think that's why he wanted you to be an apprentice."

"I wouldn't . . . I would never . . ."

"Fine, whatever. I believe you and all that crap," he says, sauntering over to the typewriter. "But I'll still have to tell mom and dad. They can sort this out way better than I could."

"Please don't. I've got nothing going for me," I plead. "You saw the ceremony. I was humiliated."

"Look, I might be willing to negotiate. You get me one of those yellow drawing sticks . . ."

"Pencils," I interrupt.

"Yeah, those. Get me two of them and I won't say anything."

"Deal," I offer a handshake, but he waves me away and turns back to the typewriter.

I sprint past Gwynn's Galloping Unicorn Utopia. The keeper shakes his fist at me. "You're startling my babies."

"I'm not sure they're babies," I say, gasping for breath.

"Well, they're skittish. After that giant metal dragon yesterday."

"Sorry sir," I say dropping my jog to a speed-walk.

Bezaudorf exudes an eerie silence. Even the phonographs at Ella Vader Music Store are quiet. Across the street, the typically chatty witches gather outside of Smells Like Bundt (the only store spared in the attack) and pick at their pastries in silence. A small group of banjos lean back Wallybomber's Toy Store – where even the most frenetic toy remains motionless.

I sprint toward the Sedentary Cemetery. A flock of mobile messages interrupt the silence as they flap around toward Scary Hairy Gary the Apothecary. No one died and yet the village feels lifeless.

I sprint through the graveyard, dodging headstones along the way. A stray ghost swirls past me and warns me to "show some respect." I'm not trying to be disrespectful. I just want to help build a robot. As I reach the catacomb, a jolt shoots up my spine.

"Take me there," a girl whispers.

"I wasn't doing anything," I say.

"Wendell? Why are . . ." I turn around to see Sarah standing there with her wand aimed at my throat.

"It's not what it looks like," I say.

"Take me there," she demands.

"I don't know what you're talking about." I shake my head.

"I can tell when you're lying, Wendell. I won't say anything. I promise. Just take me to the DUMP."

"Okay, but we have to go now to avoid the zombies."

She trails behind. "Are you singing 'Twinkle Twinkle Little Star' right now?"

"Humming, actually," I point out. "And you interrupted me." Suddenly, I've lost my pace. Mildred said it was a straight shot, but there's a part where it veers slightly, right before the crazy maze of zombies. Is this it right here?

"You do know where we're going, right?"

"Yeah," I mumble. Three zombies growl at us from across the chamber. Sarah sprints – not away from them, but straight toward them. I close my eyes as they raise their torches and howl. I push forward with a sudden burst. A thunderous crash echoes across the catacombs. More screaming. Something pulls on my robe. Opening my eyes, I see Sarah.

"Let's go," she says, tugging my robe again. We turn the corner and dart across the chambers, tumbling through the wobbly bridge.

I shriek when we land in the chasm.

"Oh please, Wendell, they're not poisonous. Look at this," she says, holding the snake up to my face. Somehow that doesn't help. She follows me through the tunnel and jumps out of the shrubbery.

"So this is it," she says, pointing to the DUMP.

I nod.

"I always wondered if it was a different dimension, but look at the sun," she points at a small orb in the fog. "It's positioned exactly like our side."

Really? She is now in the DUMP and all she can pay attention to is the sun?

"Hey Sarah, why are you so interested in the DUMP?"

Nothing. She's too absorbed in the moment to notice me.

"Why did you turn down every school that offered a banner?"

Again, nothing. "It looks just like I imagined, only foggier."

"Oh no, that's not fog. That's the mystical mist," I say. "Apparently it's how the winter works here in Fresssno."

She furrows her eyebrows and heads toward the sidewalk. Phil meets us with a goofy grin. "You made it. You really made it."

"This is Phil," I point out. "He works with robots."

"Hey, you brought a friend," Phil says. Instinctively, she pulls out her wand and aims it at his temple.

"Right, you're a wizard, too" he laughs.

"A witch," she corrects him. "Um, I mean, I'm dressed like a witch."

"Nice wand. Where'd you buy it?"

"Wanda's Wand Emp . . . Wait, a minute." She turns to me and places her wand in her pocket. "Did you tell him about the enchanted world?"

"No, it's cool. I get it. You're into dressing up, too. You're pretending to be a magical couple. It's cool." He winks at her.

"I'm not with him," she says.

"But you guys came here together?"

"Yeah, but . . ."

"Are you here to help us with the robot?" he asks.

She shakes her head. "I've got other plans, actually. I've been looking for this place for a long time."

He shrugs his shoulders as she walks down the sidewalk. Turning around, she points to him. "You said your name is Phil?"

"Well, my family calls me Junior, but everyone else calls me Phil."

"And you work on robots?"

"Of course," he says.

"I'll do it, then." She holds out her hand to shake it and he slaps it.

"What was that for?" she snarls.

"That's a high five. Wizards don't do that?"

"No, we don't. And I'm not a wizard. I'm a witch."

As we walk toward his house, Sarah peppers him with questions. "So, is salsa a dance or a condiment?"

"It's both," he says.

"And you solve problems with thumb wars, right?"

"They're more like thumb skirmishes or maybe thumb battles. It's never truly a war."

"Oh my Merlin, I love this place," she says with a grin.

As we walk into the house, Sarah darts to the kitchen and points to the black box.

"Wait? You have a microwave?" she gasps.

"That's pretty standard," Phil says.

"We had one when we were little. You just push the button and then your food is ready?"

"Well, it has to be in a dish first."

She grabs a metal pan and tosses it inside. "Ooh, pop corn." She taps the button. Sparks fly.

Phil sprints to the kitchen and opens the microwave door.

His mom runs in from the bedroom with a scowl. "Junior, have you been trying to microwave soap again?"

"It wasn't me, I swear."

Sarah steps forward. "I'm sorry, ma'am. I'm not from around here and, see, I didn't . . . I didn't know how they work."

Phil's mom furrows her eyebrows. "Where are you from, then?"

"I'm from a small village in the echant . . . in the region of Enchantistan. We don't have microwaves. We use cauldrons."

"Well, next time ask permission. That's our third microwave in two years," she adds, staring at Phil.

As we head over to Phil's room, Sarah studies an old family picture.

"Is that your father?" she asks.

"My parents are divorced, but she still keeps the family picture up," Phil explains.

"Interesting," she says.

We walk into the room and instantly Sarah jumps on the computer and starts typing some kind of foreign language filled with dots and colons and short words that I can't begin to comprehend.

"Your code is all messed up," she says. "I'm surprised you were able to get that thing to do anything. Maybe I should be the programmer instead. If we're going to have a shot at this contest, you'll need . . ."

"You know code? I thought you said you were a magician," Phil points out.

"No, not a magician. Nor a wizard. I'm a witch," she says with a smirk.

"But you know how to program?"

"My dad was a smuggler to the DUMP."

"He was a dumpster diver?"

"No, he went into the non-magical world and bought things. When I was little, we had a computer. They got rid of it after he died. But I kept the books of code and studied them in my spare time. I have a gnome friend who lets me practice on his computer sometimes."

Phil goes over the details of the competition. It starts with a review by judges. After that, the real competition starts. Our robot has to make it through a previously unknown obstacle course grabbing flags along the way.

After an hour, we come to the conclusion that we're going to start out from scratch if we have a chance at winning the contest. So, we plan out our ideas for how the robot will win in the speed, agility, originality and functionality categories. I sit back quietly while both of them argue about the details.

"You're wizards . . ."

"I'm a witch," she interrupts.

"Yeah, yeah, I know. So, I was thinking . . . what if we made it a robotic dragon? That would be different," Phil points out.

"Or a jet. You don't know anyone who knows how jets work?" Sarah says.

"My dad does, but I want to design it ourselves. Besides, drones are dull. I want to make a dragon."

"But your dad knows about jets?"

"Why are you so focused on my dad?"

"I'm just looking for any edge that might help us win," she says.

"We're not going to ask for his help," Phil says.

"So, about the dragon," I interrupt. "Would it breathe fire?"

"It could. But it could also do voice recognition and send messages and . . . I don't know, make someone a cappuccino or a latte. I mean, we would leave that up to the person ordering it."

We sketch out our plans and begin assembling the parts. It doesn't look like a dragon so much as a mechanical angry bird (which, according to Phil, you're supposed to hurl at pigs). Still, it's a start. The base remains too heavy and the wings flap awkwardly, but after a few hours, we are getting closer to a dragonbot.

"Hey, you left these in the family room and now it smells like a skunk sprayed a dead ocelot," Phil's sister says, tossing a pair of cleats that career off the desk and shatter the robot.

Sarah pulls out her wand and cries, "Stop the velocity with all due ferocity, all stands still to stop the atrocity."

Instantly, the pieces stand still in the air. Phil's eyes light up. "Th-th-th . . . this is real."

I nod.

"You were right. She's right. It's all . . . real."

His sister darts down the hall. "Mom, they're doing sorcery in the bedroom."

"Oh, honey, there's nothing going on. I've told you before that magic isn't real."

"No, mom. The robot is stuck in the air," she says, tugging on her mom's shirt.

Waving her wand, Sarah adds, "Reverse the inertia so all will be fixed. Let the shattering end and destruction be nixed."

The pieces flitter about, still suspended in air.

"Speed it up," I say.

Sarah remains silent.

"Make it go faster," I add.

Sarah shakes her head, eyes still fixated on the robotic pieces.

"Mom, this is real. You have to come see it for yourself."

"I'll check it out," I can hear his mom say from the kitchen.

The wings straighten out. Intricate pieces click back into place. However, the frame remains extended in mid-air.

"Can't you speed this up?" I ask.

"It's a slow spell, because I had to use a slant rhyme in 'reverse the inertia.' I should have used the standard spell, but it just kind-of slipped. And now it's too late."

"Why can't we just grab it?" Phil asks.

I shake my head. "Don't get in the way of this spell. Wizards have been petrified for days when they miss with this."

"Really?" Phil's eyes light up.

"It's rare, but it happens."

I listen to the pattering of feet as Phil's mom crosses the family room and heads toward the hallway, chiding her daughter for making up fanciful tales. The second wing straightens out. Tiny gears slip back into place lethargically.

"Hey, you're not doing magic, right?" she hollers from the hallway.

"That's impossible. I'm a man of science. Or, a boy of silence," Phil says, blocking the doorway. "But Genevieve almost ruined our robot when she threw my cleats at it."

"Let's take a look," she says, pushing him out of the way. Right then, the wings click into the frame as it glides to the table.

"Oh, sweetheart, that's not magic. That's better than magic. That's engineering. And you can be an engineer when you're older."

Minutes later, Phil asks to see the wand.

"It won't work if you're not magical. I'm sorry, but that's just how it is," Sarah says.

"Then what's the harm?" he asks.

"Go on, but don't be disappointed when it won't work."

"Oopsy daisy, nifty drifty, my slacks' waistline will now be fifty."

"Like that's really going to work. You have to concentrate and . . ." she begins. But it's too late. His pants are already massive. He has to hold them up with his left hand.

None of us can believe what just happened. He did it. Phil used a wand and did magic without needing any practice.

She shakes her head. "Wait, wait. Oopsy daisy? Nifty drifty? Slacks? What are you, eighty years old?"

"I'm sorry," Phil says. "I just thought that wizards used a lot of old language. See, watch this: Puffy duffy, this is dandy, my pillow case is full of candy."

His whole bed vibrates. The walls shake. He drops the wand and grabs the pillowcase.

"Licorice? Does anyone younger than my grandpa like licorice?" he complains, as the pieces fly across the room.

"See, that's what you get for using words like 'dandy.' Spells will react to it," Sarah points out.

"It's got to be some kind of remote control," he says. "There's no such thing as magic."

Sarah shakes her head. "Are your parents magical?"

"Not that I know of," he says.

I snatch the wand and aim it at his lizard. "I hold it up and place it down, this green lizard will now be brown."

The lizard dives down and lands on the wand. It works. Not instantly, but over time his reptilian friend goes from green to brown.

"I did it! I made the wand work!" I say loud enough that even his mother peeks in.

"Ahem, sorry to inform you of this, but that's camouflage. Lenny does that with any stick."

"I know. I was just messing around." I try not to act disappointed, but it's hard being the only firt in the room.

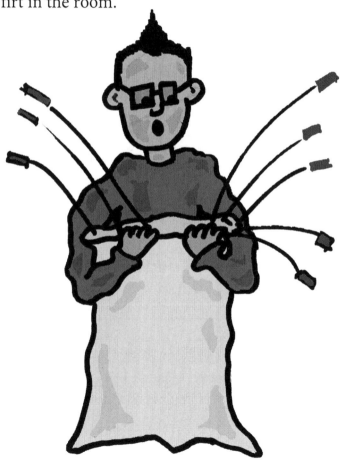

However, things change when we go back to the robot. For the second day in a row, I get lost in the design and realize, only when the sun is setting, that's time to leave. The catacombs are still terrifying, but I leave with a rush of adrenaline and the hopes of building something that might just win the competition.

I arrive home just short of dinnertime. Apparently the Misfits let a massive silver dragon loose over Restaurant Row.

"They say it was so fast you couldn't see the wings move," my dad says.

"I think it was a machine," Greg says. "I think the Misfits are building an army. The guys at Holland Oats Man Eatery said that it roared when it flew by. Scared all their customers away."

"Customers? Nobody's liked Holland Oats since in the eighties."

"Do you think the Misfits will attack our castle?" Melissa asks.

My mom shakes her head as she passes the chocolate-covered pumpkin seeds. "Let's talk about something happier, shall we? Benny stopped by and said that the job offer is still there for you."

"I'll think about it," I mutter. I want to speak up. I want to tell my mom that Benny might be behind the attacks; that recruiting me is part of his plan for terrorizing Bezaudorf. I want to tell her that Greg shouldn't go in the carriage if the Misfits are planning an attack on Saturday.

"Though he did say something odd. He mentioned going to the library and never running into you."

"Well, he's short, so he can't exactly see over the shelves," I explain.

"It's a good thing you were at the library today," my dad says. "You missed all of the commotion."

"Y-y-yeah, i-i-it is," I stammer.

"Funny you mention that. I thought it closed early on Sundays," my mom says.

"It does. I mean, for everyone else. But they let me stay since I'm researching potential apprenticeships," I explain. "Nerdy Nick feels bad for me, because I'm a firt."

"I'll have to send him a thank you note. It's not every librarian . . ."

"It's okay. You don't need to. I mean, I'd rather be the one to send the thank you note."

Later that night as I slide into my makeshift bed, Greg sends a mobile message flying through my drafty window, "Twenty-four pencils tomorrow or I'm telling mom and dad."

I pull out my parchment and begin sketching out a new wing design for our robot dragon. I'd love a pencil, but instead I'm using the vomit-scented marker from Benny's Bored Games. One by one, my family settles down and goes to sleep while I continue to sketch out the plans.

I lean up against my sleeping dragon and try to imagine the flight pattern. The wings are too heavy and we're getting no lift. Not even a tiny bit. It hobbles around pretty well and we were able to get the claws to grasp at a straw on the first try. But with only two and a half days left, it feels far outside of our reach.

ELEVEN
ENGINEERING IS MAGIC

It's still dark when I head out of my castle, with just enough light to show the steam dancing off the ground. I stray from the cobblestone road and curve around Andy Waywego Travel Brooms (a massive property poorly placed next to the Bezaudorf Jail).

Yesterday's eerie silence is now replaced by the pounding of hammers and smashing of dishes at Clark's Cobbler. Sweet Treat Tweet Street is still slick with burnt sugar. Half the buildings are held up by little more than a charm and some imagination. Still, it's open and that's all that matters on a winter morning.

I stop by Smells Like Bundt and order a cinnamon roll and a mug of hot butterscotch.

Images of screaming villagers float off the newspaper pages that are strewn all over the tables. It's not a long walk to the police precinct. I could tell them everything I know. Then again, they probably wouldn't believe me. Benny's a hero in our village.

I try eating slowly, but I'm too anxious. I want to win this competition. So, I'm putting the *fast* back into breakfast, stuffing half the roll in my mouth. I grab my plate, hurl it at the wall and watch it shatter. The tiny pieces re-collect and begin forming a new mug. You've got to love recycling.

I pace around the Sedentary Cemetery until I can't take it anymore. It's still five until seven, but I need to go. I have a robot to build and pencils to find and this village still feels depressing. I know it's not eight, but maybe I could get a head start. I step into the entrance of the dusty catacombs. My steps echo. A chill runs up my spine and I shriek.

"Wendell," a voice whispers. A light flickers and instantly I recognize Mildred.

"What are you doing here?" I ask.

"I do have quite a business reclaiming items from the DUMP. I need to show you something," she says. "It'll only take a minute."

I follow her through the corridors. Right at the moment that I can't orient myself, she stops and turns a knob. Why doesn't she just wave her wand?

"I've been tracking the Misfits," she says, pointing to a map. "And I need your help."

"What are you talking about?"

"Let's start with Benny. He hasn't made you any offers has he?"

"Um, no," I lie.

"Wendell, this is really important. I get the sense that he is trying to attack and I know that you are the only one who can stop him. I have my reasons to believe that Filbert is alive and Benny is working with him. I think Filbert's death was a fraud."

"Well, I can't do anything to help."

"Listen, Wendell, that prophecy wasn't false. I later faked being drunk to protect you. But this is your moment. You can choose to ignore me, but this is your destiny."

I shake my head. "I'm not magical."

"We need to design something to stop them. The elves won't cooperate, but you . . . well . . . you have skills that we need."

"I appreciate it, but I'm kind-of working on something else."

"You don't have to answer yet. But just consider it. You could be heroic."

She walks me through the catacombs, dodging zombies along the way. It's a different route, free of the wobbly bridge and the tunnel, but I enter into the DUMP and step into the same mist, not far from the park.

I spend the next hour and a half waiting for Sarah. I pull out my parchment and sketch a few more adjustments to the robots as I shiver on the cold concrete bench, rubbing my hands together and wishing for a heating charm.

Finally, at half past eight Sarah pushes through the shrubs and approaches me sheepishly.

"Sorry, I'm late," Sarah says. "I had to take care of my parents."

"I don't get it. What exactly is there to do if your parents are already ghosts?"

"Never use that term."

"What?"

"Ghosts. It's an insult. They prefer the term post-living. And to answer your question, they still need my help."

"With what?"

"Lots of stuff. Reading for one. They can't turn the pages. Their hands just go straight through. So, I have to turn the pages. And letters. They can't read letters. Anyway, it's almost nine," she says. So we walk through the neighborhood quietly.

"So, Mildred thinks the attacks are from the Misfits. She thinks Filbert's still alive. What exactly did your parents see when the Misfits attacked them?"

"They've never talked about it."

"Never?"

"I'm not allowed to bring up Filbert at home."

Phil steps forward. "Filbert who?" Startled, I shriek like a four-year-old girl.

"I don't know. He's just Filbert. He's a wizard that went rogue," Sarah says.

"What do you mean went rogue?"

"Well, he was a firt, you know, a wizard who couldn't do magic. And he ran away to the du . . . the non-magical world. Nobody heard from him after awhile. Secretly he was building an army called the Misfits. About five years ago he attacked the village and killed my parents," she says. "People think it was a robotic dragon."

"Why'd he do that?" Phil asks.

"That's the crazy thing about it. We don't know. He used to work with my mom. They smuggled stuff from the DUMP. But he died. He tried attacking a gnome named Benny and he died in an explosion."

"And his name is Filbert?"

"*Was* Filbert. He's not alive anymore," I point out.

"What if Filbert wasn't really a bad guy?" Phil asks.

"Are you serious? He killed my parents. He terrorized our village. He was the most wanted wizard in all of Bezaudorf. Benny tracked him down and saved us."

"What if it's the gnome's fault? What if Filbert was framed because he was a firt?" Phil asks.

"It doesn't matter," I point out. "Filbert's dead. And speaking of dead, I'll be dead if I don't get some pencils. I promised I would find twenty-four of them for Greg and I have no idea how I'll make that happen."

"I have a few bucks. We'll just go get some over there," he says, pointing to the large red bulls-eye.

"No way. That's where the giants do target practice," I point out. "I'm not stepping anywhere near that place."

"What are you talking about? The Giants are in San Francisco. Or New York, I guess, if you're thinking of football."

"Football?"

"It's a game with tackling and end zones and stuff."

"Remind me to stay out of New York," I say, imagining enormous giants sending people to their "end zone" and making "footballs" out of their victims' feet.

We meander through the docked carriages and approach the entrance. As I step toward it, the door opens.

"Did you see it?" I yell out to Sarah. She walks forward and the door opens. She steps back and it closes, then forward and it opens again.

"What kind of magic is this?" she asks.

"You don't even have to say a spell," I point out.

"A spell? You don't even have to speak," she says. "I wonder if we can make our robot like that!"

I run up to a woman pushing a metal cart. "Have you seen the doors on this thing? They open on their own. No handles or anything."

"Yes, they do," she says, scurrying away. Sarah runs toward the Customer Service booth. "Nicely done with the doors. They opened without needing any help."

"Yes, well they tend to do that," the man says with a grin.

As I turn toward Phil, I notice a bearded man staring at me. It's no big deal. Half the store is staring at us. But he looks familiar.

"Was that Mr. Oglesby?" Sarah asks.

"Why would he be in the DUMP?" I ask.

She shakes her head. "You're right."

"Come on," Phil says, tapping Sarah on the shoulder. We follow him through the dizzying display of lights and sounds that we never experience in Bezaudorf.

I manage to look disenchanted, except in the Menswear section (which apparently isn't a place to swear at men). Twice, I notice the same bearded man peering from behind the aisles.

"I think that was Mr. Oglesby. He just wasn't wearing his robes," Sarah whispers again.

"He wasn't wearing his robes? Are you saying he was naked?" Phil whispers back.

Sarah shakes her head in disgust. When we reach the Office Supply section, Phil not only buys a pack of pencils, but he also picks up a pencil sharpener and pens (which are like quills, but don't require any ink-dipping). We leave the store with a shiny plastic bag and a guarantee that Greg will stay quiet for a few days.

"Do you hear that?" Sarah asks.

A high-pitch sound pierces the air.

"I know what that is," she says. "It's a music truck. My dad told me about ice cream trucks, but this is even better. It's a healthier option. Gets people up and moving."

"That's not a music truck," Phil says.

"Sure it is," she points out. "The repetitive sound you're hearing is called techno music. I've read all about it. Look, there are some dancers dressed in matching outfits."

"That's a fire truck," Phil says. Sure enough, the dance team runs up to the building and sets it on fire.

"They're burning it down!" I yell.

"No, they're putting it out," Phil says.

Sarah winces. "I think Wendell's right. I'm pretty sure they're setting it on fire. Look at the blaze."

"Trust me. I live here. They're firefighters. Their job is to stop the fire," Phil says.

The fire people pull out a giant water hose and spray it at the flames. Maybe Phil is right.

"See, they're pouring water on the flames," Phil says.

"No they're not. That's gas. I've read about it. It's a highly flammable clear liquid," Sarah says. "Those people are trying to destroy the building."

"That's water," Phil says.

"I'm telling you, it's gas."

"I've passed a lot of gas," I point out. "And I'm pretty sure that's water."

"We should go," Phil says. "We have a robot to work on."

"Are you joking? We have to stop them," she argues.

"You're not allowed to do magic in the DUMP. Don't you realize that you could go on trial for this?" I ask.

"There are people in there and this gang of fire people are burning the place down. Don't you feel . . ."

"Let's leave," Phil says. "We need to get our dragon to fly."

It's too late. Sarah is sprinting around the carriages, past the protesting firefighters and right into the middle of the fray. Pointing her wand, she says:

> Let the clouds formulate
> In full anticipation
> And hence change the state
> To a full precipitation

A swirling cloud forms around her wand, twirling upward and then diving down toward the building followed by an earsplitting thunder rattles the ground. Even the cars beep and howl in fear.

"Those are just car alarms," Phil says.

"Well, the cars look pretty alarmed," I admit.

A downpour drenches the building. Two firefighters continue to spray at the building, but it's pointless. The place is soaked. Shoppers gather around, gawking at the cloud and pulling out their phones. The bearded man pulls out a phone of his own and aims it at Sarah.

"This is bad. This is real bad," I whisper. "They have proof of her magic."

Phil looks at me skeptically. "Isn't there some kind of magic fog you put on people to hide your world? You know, something to make them forget."

"Nope. There's no such thing as memory charms or reality-changers. Magic only goes so far. If we're found out, we're found out."

Sarah crosses her arms and continues to aim at the fire. A larger crowd gathers, gawking at the cloud. Finally, Sarah turns away and the cloud dissipates.

"Do you realize what you just did?" I ask.

She points to three people wrapped up in blankets. "I saved their lives and the building."

"People captured that in a motion picture," I point out.

"I see what you're saying, but they were all recording the cloud."

"Yeah, but you're in every one of those motion pictures."

"Don't worry," she says calmly.

"You could go to prison for this. You know they play that annoying perky fairy music all day long. Plus, you'd be away from your parents," I point out.

"Nobody saw it start. All they saw was a crazy cloud. If they noticed me – and I doubt that they even saw me – they would have seen a kid with a stick and nothing more."

"I'm just worried about you, that's all. You had a close call yesterday and . . ."

She points her finger in my face. "Worried? The only thing you should be worried about is finishing this robot. The contest is in two days and you still can't get it to fly. How about you worry about that instead?"

"Got it," I gulp.

TWELVE
THE SPARE PART

Between the nightmares of the Misfits and the guilt about not talking to Greg about Saturday, I didn't sleep more than an hour last night. Even when I tried sketching out plans for the dragon, I ended up with a pile of crumpled up parchment..

So here I am at Phil's house, fighting to keep my eyes open. It's not that I'm bored. It's just that the whole thing feels bigger than anything we can accomplish. Sarah's staring at a screen while Phil fiddles with wires.

"What should we name him?" I ask.

"Why does our robot have to be a him?" Sarah points out.

"How about Denny the Dragon?" I suggest.

Phil points at the dragon. "No, no, no. People always go with alliteration. That's so cliché. Let's name her something no one expects, like Fran. It could be an acronym for Flying Robotic . . ."

"We're not naming him Fran," I protest. "Other robots have names like the Turbobot 2000."

"No, I like Fran. Let's go with it," Sarah says.

I glare at both of them. "You have to have a number, though," I point out. "Every robot has a number at the end."

"Pi is a great number," Phil says. "It goes on forever."

"I like that. Fran Pi it is," Sarah says.

"That might be the worst robot name ever," I protest. "I was thinking Dragobot or Robodragon or . . ." but I can see that they're not listening.

Sarah changes the subject, "Wendell, you haven't figured out the flight stuff yet."

"True, but I got the neck working. Look how fast it moves." I flip the switch and watch Fran Pi crane her neck. It's still choppy, but it's fast.

"A dragon is supposed to fly. I thought you said you would work on it last night."

"I *did* work on it last night. I was up until two in the morning. It's not like you got the fire to work. I thought you were supposed to fix the fire issues."

How to Name a Robot

Option One: Robo-Noun

Formula: The + Robo+noun + Number

The Robokoalocelot 3140:
It's a bird! No, that's not even close. It's a robot!
It's a koala! It's an ocelot! No, it's the
Robokoalocelot 3140!

The Robocatpirate 600:
Arr! He be very fur-strated right meow.

The Robotub 9000:
This one was a bust.
Turns out rubber duckies are safer
for kids than bath-time robots.

OPTION TWO: ADJECTIVE-BOT
Formula: The + Adjective+bot + Number

The Smellybot 9100:
Some robots are gas-powered.
Others have powerful gas.

Meh.

The Apathybot 4500:
This robot has the ability
to destroy things with its
lasers and fly across the
neighborhood in seconds, but . . .
it just doesn't care.

OPTION THREE: VERBINATOR
Formula: The + Verb + inator + Number

The Knitinator:
This robot was designed by
Scarf Ace ("Say hello to my little friend").
He takes knitting to a whole new level.

The Flossinator 2800:
Nobody likes to floss.
However, that doesn't stop this robot
from flossing everyone in sight.

She glares at me. "I only took that on because you couldn't get it to work. I'm supposed to be programming, remember? Besides, I had another project to work on."

"More important than this project?" I ask.

"Yeah, it kind of is. You wouldn't understand, though."

"What? Because it requires magic? Is this about me being a firt?"

"When have I ever given you a hard time about being disenchanted?"

Phil steps in. "I'm going to go out on a limb here and suggest that maybe this dragon doesn't need to make cappuccinos."

Ignoring him, I turn to Sarah. "I think alcohol was a bad idea. We need a different liquid for the fire. What was that stuff you mentioned before? Gas?"

"Gas is too dangerous. What about lighter fluid?" Phil asks.

"Anything will work better than what we've got," I point out.

"Magic is what we really need," Sarah says.

I shake my head. "That's too risky. You saw what happened yesterday."

"Nobody found out," Sarah says.

"But they could have," I point out. "Did you see all the people taking motion pictures of it?"

She shrugs. "If only we had access to the elves. They'd know how to make the wings work."

"Wait, so elves are real, too?" Phil asks.

I jump from my chair. "That's it. We don't know elves, but we do know someone who worked for them."

I pack up my satchel and head out the door. However, as I walk through the neighborhood, this idea suddenly seems insane. If Benny was behind the attacks a couple of days ago – which all evidence suggests he is – it feels like I'm barging in on the enemy. My hands shake and I find myself speed walking through the park and toward the shrubbery at the entrance of the catacombs.

I turn back and take a deep breath. I slip in, glide through the tunnel and wait for the bridge to drop. The torchlight bounce off stone ceilings, creating manic shadows. I'm jumpy, but I manage to creep through the first chamber unnoticed.

I still can't make sense out of Sarah. Why does she care so much about this project if she's also working on something else? What was she looking for in the DUMP and why did she abandon that just to join us?

I slip through the final corridor and out into the Sedentary Cemetery. Mildred's stand is empty, which means I won't have to explain why I'm sneaking around.

After putting on my robe, I march toward the Town Tetrahedron. It's louder now, with the self-propelled banjos bursting out in song. Children are giggling at the new Whirling Wixies dancing around the windows of Wallybomber's Toy Store while a group of young witches chase after an escaped schnorbitz disk that zipped out of Scott's Sports Shop unannounced. A few bakeries are still blackened and covered with ash, but Bezaudorf is starting to feel normal again.

Even the typically stodgy clerks at Taylor's Tailor leave the childish graffiti charm alone. The sign changes from "Get Your Fancy Button Here" to "Get Your Fancy Butt On Here" when you pass by the street.

The clerk at Panarese Panoramic Pictures Palace dodges a flying delivery of canned meat.

"It's just spam," he says as a stray can bounces off his forehead.

"Keep it," his wife says. "I'm planning on making a fake meat statue." Okay, maybe the term "normal" doesn't apply to our village.

I dart past the floating images at Ratkovic's Relics and head toward the Gnome Home. This is it. I'm walking straight into the enemy's lair. I duck down and open the door.

"Is Benny here?" I ask.

The waitress nods and points toward the backroom, where Benny meets me with a shady grin. It doesn't look particularly shady. It actually looks pretty genuine. However, everything about him now feels shady. He's got that super-villain vibe going for him.

"I've been waiting for you," he says. "Are you thinking of joining us?"

"Well, not really. I was actually hoping I could borrow one of the small dragons you used to make when you worked for the elves."

He strokes his beard. "You came here to buy a defunct toy?"

"Yeah, well, I'm bored," I lie.

He pulls his wand out and aims it at the door, slamming it shut without so much as a curse.

"Why are you really here?" he asks.

"I . . . uh . . . I'm . . . bored."

He shakes his head and leans forward. He might be small, but it feels as if he's towering over me. "What do you need it for?"

"I like to build stuff. I want to see if I can make a dragon of my own."

"The dragons have been banned from Bezaudorf," he points out. "They were supposed to be destroyed. How did you know about them?"

My stomach sinks.

"I asked you a question," he says.

I can't speak. I can't move. Well, that's not entirely true. My whole body is shaking.

He glares at me again. "What all did you see in my basement?" I shake my head.

"I gave you a chance, Wendell. On two occasions, I gave you ample opportunity to choose. It's not too late. You can get your revenge on the village. Prove to them what you're really made of. You can build things bigger than a tiny dragon robot."

"I . . . I . . . I should go."

"Nonsense," he says.

"I'm just going to . . ."

"Who sent you?" he snarls. "It was Mildred, was it not?"

I cough. "Nobody sent me. I just wanted to get a spare part, I swear."

He aims his wand at a beaker. It shatters, spilling a luminescent lavender liquid on the desk. I watch it sizzle as it falls to the ground.

"I would hate to see anyone - especially a good kid like you - get in the way of our mission."

He aims his wand in the opposite direction. A metal dragon falls from a bookcase and swoops down toward us. Without the slightest incantation, the wings pop off and the creature falls to the ground. I cringe as it wriggles on the ground and howls in pain.

"Relax. It's an inanimate object," he says, as the pieces crumble into a pile.

"Looks pretty animated to me."

"You need the whole thing?"

"Just the wings."

"If anyone asks, Mildred sold these to you. Deal?"

"Deal," I whisper. I stuff the wings inside my satchel.

"Would you like to stay and have a hot butterscotch?"

"No thanks."

"Are you sure? We have the best hot butterscotch in all of Bezaudorf. Beats that watered-down sewage drink they sell at Smells Like Bundt."

"I'm good."

"It's on me," he says, pouring the miniature mug on his shirt.

"Thanks, but I have a robot to build."

"For the contest," he says with a wink. "Good luck."

I dart through the village and head to the Sedentary Cemetery. How does he know so much? Does he have a spy working for him?

Without much thought, I step into the catacombs and jog through the corridors.

"What are you doing here?" a boy says, holding a wand to my face. The stick is jostling. He seems nervous.

"Aren't you going to do a light charm?" I ask just as nervously.

"I'm g-g-g-good with the d-d-dark. I'll let the authorities look at you when I bring you in."

"Wait a second, that's not a wand, is it? That's just a twig."

"No. It's a wand, I swear," he says.

"Then do a spell."

"I can't. I'm a firt. Just like you," he says. The catacombs, the dark, the lack of magic. Suddenly it makes sense. "You're a . . . You're a zombie," I say.

"Come with me," he whispers.

"Please don't eat my brains out," I implore. I jump forward and notice a flickering light of zombie guards pacing back and forth.

"This way," he whispers, tugging on my shirt. I follow him through a maze of corridors, dodging the zombies along the way. He grabs a torch from the wall and leads me into a narrow passageway.

"Please don't eat my brains," I beg.

He laughs. I can't tell if it's friendly or maniacal. "I won't eat your brains. I'm actually brain-intolerant. Now, minds are different. I'm always interested in those. You won't find a zombie kid that reads more than I do," he says.

"So, you're not going to eat my brains?"

He grabs a torch and then adjusts his glasses. "Besides, zombies don't eat human brains. They eat cow brains."

"That's disgusting," I say.

"It's no worse than a hot dog," he says.

"Do you eat the brains raw?"

"I don't eat it at all, remember? I'm brain-intolerant. I get hives if I eat a raw brain. But, yeah, most zombies are raw foodies. We just happen to be carnivores, too." He hands me a pamphlet from the Council of Counsel.

"You make it sound normal."

"It is . . . to us. Anyway, we don't have much time. I need to talk to you about something."

"Go on," I say.

He's shaking. Not a little bit, but enough that he's about to light my robe on fire.

"Well, it's complicated," he says. "But someone sent me to talk to you."

"Who sent you?"

"I can't say," he says.

"Just let me know. I'll keep it a secret," I plead.

Five Things You Probably Didn't Know About Zombies

(But You Would Know If You Bothered to Get to Know One Of Them; Which, Of Course, You Wouldn't Do If You Were Scared They'd Eat Your Brains Out.)

Myth #1: Zombies Will Eat Your Brains

Zombies do eat brains. Raw brains. I know, gross. However, just think of it like eating a raw hot dog. I know. Still pretty gross. But not evil at least. Unless you're a cow.

Myth #2: Zombies Have Bad Posture

Okay, this one is a little complicated to explain. By human standards, yes, their posture is pretty bad. Atrocious, actually. However, that's an unfair accusation. That's like a fairy complaining about human flight.

BY THE COUNCIL OF COUNSEL

Myth #3: The Living Dead

Often people believe that zombies can't die. Not true at all. Where they differ from us is that they shed their skin (and entire body parts). Consider it turbo-charged exfoliating with a slightly reptilian twist.

Myth #4: Slow Zombies

When you see rows of zombies muttering slowly with arms outstretched, chances are it's just the elderly zombies doing calisthenics.

Myth #5: Zombies Are Always Angry

Most of the whole "angry zombie" thing comes from the fact that they speak German and Germans always sound angry, even when they wish you a good day.

He shakes his head. "Everything you know is wrong. The Misfits aren't who you think they are and neither is Filbert."

"*Was* Filbert," I correct him.

He shakes his head. "Benny isn't who you think he is, either."

"I know. I know all about Benny."

"Well, there's more. It's about the Misfits. You need to know that they . . ."

"Charles?" a woman's voice echoes. He hands me the torch and flips out a key ring. His hands are shaking so badly he can't identify the right key.

"Charles?" the voice echoes louder. I glance at the dancing shadows.

"Just breathe," I warn him, but he's hyperventilating, circling through the keys.

"Take it," I whisper, handing him the torch. He jumps out into the chambers while I crouch down in the corner of the filthy room.

"Hey, mom. I got lost," he says.

"Who were you talking to?" she asks, waving her torch around. I keep my eyes shut (as though my inability to see her will keep her from seeing me).

"No one, mom."

"I heard whispering."

"That was the wind," he adds. Their voices fade into the background. I have to get out of here. I feel around in the dark for the keys. I run my hand over the cold stone and clutch them the moment I hear them jangle.

"What was that?" she asks.

"Probably just a rat, mom."

"I'm checking," she says. I jump to my feet and feel around for a keyhole. I jangle each key as the bouncing light grows brighter.

"I hear it still," she says. Finally, the key slips in. I twist it and push the door through, tumbling into the DUMP. I stumble around the sidewalk trying my best to orient myself. I see the park in the distance and the huge lit-up bulls-eye not far from here.

"Come on! What took you so long?" Sarah yells. I look around, but I can't see her.

"Over here, Dragon Booger Boy!" she yells. I hardly recognize her in jeans and a purple hooded sweatshirt.

As we sit on a curb, I tell her everything about Benny and the Misfits and Charles the Brain Intolerant Zombie Boy.

"Did he give you any details?"

"He didn't have time," I point out. "But I'm feeling really confused. He talked about Filbert as if he's still alive. Do you think Filbert and Benny are behind the Misfits?"

She shrugs her shoulders. "I have no idea, actually. Did he leave you any kind of clues?"

"Not really. But I did find these bad boys . . ."

She raises an eyebrow.

"Or bad girls," I continue, "The keys could be girls, I guess."

"Do you realize what this means?" she asks.

"Yep. It means the keys don't really have a specific gender," I respond.

"No, it means that we can find their lair." Her eyes look enormous right now. "We can go tomorrow night after the competition. We'll take Fran Pi and use her to spy. We just need a motion picture recorder. Maybe Phil's phone?"

I shake my head. "You don't know if their lair is in the catacombs."

"It has to be," she responds. "They're getting supplies from the DUMP and attacking out of the graveyard. Think about it. The zombies have to be on the side of the Misfits. And who can blame them? The zombies feel like misfits, too."

"But they're working with the police," I point out. "Why would they be against the village if they're working as guards?"

"Exactly. It's the perfect cover. I have my theory. I think the catacombs connect to someone's home."

"Benny's?"

"I doubt it," she says, jumping back up and shuffling down the sidewalk. We continue winding our way through the neighborhoods. Quietly we march toward Phil's house. Suddenly it clicks. Sarah's been working to stop the Misfits. That's why she wanted to find the DUMP and that's why she's so focused on the robotic dragon.

Minutes later, we're at Phil's house testing out the dragon. The new wings work perfectly. Of course they do. They're magical. However, I conveniently forget to explain that to Sarah and Phil. They're too excited about having an honest-to-goodness flying dragon.

Still, the afternoon has its glitches. The flames are hit or miss. It's not a big deal for the contest, but it drives Sarah crazy. The dragon flies perfectly, but on the downward spiral, we lose control of the claws. Sarah thinks it's mechanical, but I blame the code.

As the sun fades, I throw up my hands (not to be confused with "throw up in my hands," which would be totally different).

"This is the best we're going to do."

"I can work on it at home. Let me try to get the flames to work," Sarah says, carefully setting the dragon in her space-charmed satchel.

"I was kind-of thinking I could work on it."

She shakes her head. "No, I'll do it. Just make sure you meet up with us at nine. Don't be late."

The contest isn't until tomorrow, but I'm already nervous. I stare at Phil's empty trophy case and imagine the robot trophy staring back at us.

"I think we're going to win," I say, though I have no idea what we're up against . . . or how hard it will be to get there on time.

THIRTEEN
GRANDMA'S REVENGE

Greg yanks the covers off my bed and tosses them on Ash. "Wake up, wittle bwudder. Did you forget about grandma?"

I curl up in a ball. "It's freezing in here."

"It's not freezing. It's just cold," he says.

"No, it really is freezing in here."

He flicks his wand and mutters a Latin curse. Instantly I can see my breath. Icicles form on the ceiling. "Now it's freezing," he smiles as he walks out the door.

I shiver as I slip on a new shirt and pull on my robes. I dart down the hallway and pound on his door.

"No firts allowed," he yells.

"I need to talk to you. It's serious."

The door flies open.

"Listen, I think the Misfits are going to attack on Saturday. You have to listen to me. Don't go there."

He laughs. "You want me to ditch my carriage because you have a hunch the Misfits will attack?"

"It's not just a hunch. It's real. They're going to attack," I point out.

He glares at me. "You're not working for them, are you?"

"No, but they tried to recruit me."

"And you said no?"

"Of course I said no."

"So you're telling me that they just gave away their plans to you even though you hadn't even joined them?"

"I guess." Suddenly it sounds suspicious.

"Wendell, I think someone was messing with you. Probably Bruno. Speaking of which, I need to stop by his castle. We could use him on our schnorbitz team."

"Wendell!" my grandma screams through a charmed megaphone. When I fail to respond, she repeats it in various voices, laughing at herself in the process.

I dart down the stairs. Forget about Greg. I need to make this breakfast thing fast if I'm going to make it to the Robot Fair by nine.

As we head toward Smells Like Bundt, my grandma reminds me that I agreed to help her go grocery shopping. I'm not thrilled to be going to the grocery store with my grandma. She complains about the products and the prices and often chooses to "taste test" items that she has no intention of buying. When that's done, she has to pay with coins instead of using her wand, so a huge crowd backs up behind us.

With Baldwin's Pure Bread Bakery still out for repairs, we're stuck behind a long line. Betty has extra help in the form of a gnome and a troll. Unfortunately, the gnome can't see above the second shelf and the troll keeps insulting customers with phrases like, "Cake for breakfast? Have you seen your figure? Go get some carrot sticks."

I pull out my pocket watch as we approach the counter. It's already ten after eight. Despite the line behind us, my grandma decides to chitchat with Betty.

"I need a new hairdo," Betty says. "But the scissors are still on strike at Hairs to You Mrs. Robinson and I refuse to go to some wizard barber shop where they're going to talk about schnorbitz the whole time."

"If she would just agree to the rust protection plan, we could get our hair done," my grandma says.

"I blame the elves. I think they charmed the scissors that way just to squeeze out the rust protection plan from her. Greed is what it is."

The conversation continues as the line forms behind us. People are huffing and puffing, but it makes no difference. Betty and grandma are now talking about hair-coloring charms. I glance at my pocket watch again. Eight fifteen. Finally, I interrupt.

"Can we get some cinnamon rolls?" I cut in.

"Sure," Betty says, reaching into the display case.

After scarfing down the cinnamon rolls and watching my grandma slowly sip her coffee, I check the pocket watch again. It's eight thirty. My grandma could easily take another half an hour finishing her coffee.

"Let's go grocery shopping," I say abruptly.

"You seem awfully excited to go."

"I am. You know how I feel about food and kitchens and stuff."

"Really? I had a feeling you were interested in being a chef. It's a great career for a firt. Right Betty? Wendell here could be a baker, maybe."

"That's right!" Betty yells. "It's perfect for firts! You wouldn't have to be a misfit."

I look away, but I can feel it. Every eye in the bakery is on me.

"Well in that case, let's go check out The Pan Tree."

WENDELL THE WORLD'S WORST WIZARD

"No, it's okay. You don't have to . . ." It's too late. My grandma is already out the door and heading toward the kitchenware store housed in a massive maple tree. I glance at my pocket watch again.

It is now a quarter 'till nine. Sarah and Phil are probably at the school right now waiting for me. If I sprinted through the Sedentary Cemetery, I could make it. Or not.

"Let's take the elevator," I point out.

"I don't trust it. The charm is too old. Let's walk."

She hobbles up the spiral staircase and instantly begins waving her walking stick at the pots and pans.

"Maybe we should go to the grocery store," I point out.

"Nonsense," she says, dodging a low branch holding wrought iron utensils.

While she stares glassy-eyed at the self-cleaning cauldrons, Big Bruno Buchanan, the Ballistic Bully Boy catches a glimpse of me from the stoop outside of Barry's a Basket Case (with crazy bargains on satchels and such).

I turn away, hoping he doesn't see me. My grandma is banging on a cauldron. "They're probably aluminum or some junk. They don't make 'em like they used to."

"Please refrain from smashing our items," the clerk says.

"Smash? Oh my Merlin! See, that's the problem. If this stick can dent it then the cauldron is no good." She whacks it with her walking stick, sending a flock of birds out of the branches.

"Well, you don't have to buy it," the cashier says in a singsong voice.

"No big whoop. I was just about to go to the grocery store," she says, barging out the door and barreling down the spiral staircase.

As we walk down Sweet Treat Tweet Street, Bruno hops on his broom and zooms around us, nearly knocking my grandmother down.

We hurry past the stench of We Smell Fowl and toward the scent of apple cinnamon at Clark's Cobbler (the only place in Bezaudorf where you can get your shoes fixed while eating a slice of pie). As we saunter past Chamberlain's Charms, Bruno zips by again, hawking a mucous-packed loogie just inches away from my grandma's oversized enchanted hat.

"Did you see that?" I ask.

"See what?" she responds. As we head toward the Goerend's Grocery, I pull out my pocket watch. It's already a quarter past nine. Sarah's going to kill me.

"Grandma, do you think I could go right now? I'm supposed to meet a friend."

"Oh yeah, sure. Go on. I'm old and lonely and this is the highlight of my week. I won't be here forever. But go on, dear."

Gulp. Guess I'll be grocery shopping. A gnome greets us at Goerend's Grocery with a half-smile. He's trying his best to keep a flock of flittering coupons under control. "Go on and grab one . . . if you can catch it. It's for buy one get one free lavender floor rushes, with extra charm to push away that musty 'old castle' smell."

CHAPTER THIRTEEN

My grandma bats away a flying coupon and heads straight for the Elixir Ingredients department.

"I need a jar of pickled newt livers," she says, pointing her crooked finger at the lady behind the counter.

"You're not supposed to be making potions," the clerk points out. "It's an age thing."

"Oh, it's not for a potion. It's for dinner," she lies with a nearly toothless grin.

"Well, I can't serve you," the clerk says.

"Of course you can't serve it to me. I'd have to serve it to you. After all, I'm the one making newt liver stew. You can join me if you'd like. I'm old and lonely and I could use some company."

The clerk shakes her head and blows the dust off the jar. "If you really want to use it in a stew, I guess I can't stop you. Just promise me you won't make a potion."

"I promise," my grandma says, crossing her fingers behind her back.

"You lied to her," I whisper as we walk across the aisle.

"Nonsense. I had my fingers crossed. If she didn't notice, it's not my fault. Clerks these days. They need to pay better attention." She pulls me aside and whispers, "It's a flying potion for Ash. Only works once in a dragon's lifetime, but I think I'll give it a whirl."

As my grandma peruses the chaotic floating inked advertisements and the flittering papers of the "un-stationary stationery" display, I glance at her list and slip away to buy trash-compacting bags. Might as well speed this trip up.

I step into the cleaning aisle and immediately I'm barraged by the Pic-C Power Pixie Powder (dip your wand and amplify your cleaning power).

My eyes water. My nose itches. I sneeze and wipe my nose with my robe. More dust flitters toward me and I sneeze again. And again. I can't stop it. The sneezing fit is so bad that I nearly catch my robe on fire when I run past the pre-charmed floating candle display.

By the time I stop sneezing, I'm already at the trash-compacting bags. However, they're up at the top of a forty-two foot tall shelf. This isn't a big deal for most enchanted folk. Just a flick of the wand and the items fall straight into your satchel. If you're concerned about theft, don't be. The items are charmed to stay in the store until the clerk rings you up.

I flag down a stocker (not the hardest wizard job, given the fact that most items are self-stocking). "Excuse me sir, but I can't reach that."

He rolls his eyes while I meander the aisle pretending to be interested in self-cleaning sponges. A few minutes later, he walks back with a rickety ladder that I reluctantly climb.

As I brace the top rung on the highest shelf, a crowd forms. I might as well have a sign that reads, "Look at the firt who can't even go grocery shopping without needing help."

Bruno steps into the aisle. "This should be entertaining. Let's see if he can get the bags without screwing it up."

I climb the ladder reluctantly. It cracks with each step. I reach the top rung and stretch toward the box of bags, but all at once, the floating "Cleaning Supplies" banner twirls around my arm. I'm airborne, floating along the aisle, kicking down the Live Dust Bunnies. Suddenly the aisle is packed with fairy dust. It scatters across the store, causing the dragon toys to come alive. Squeaky squirrels scurry along the store, knocking down the dancing bags of dragon food.

I continue flying around, arm and leg tangled around the banner, riding it like an untamed magic carpet, knocking down jars of Royal Flush (charmed to keep your porcelain throne clean, respectable and free of clogs).

I catch a glimpse of Bruno hiding his wand under his robe. With a quick flick, he catapults me toward the Apothecary aisle. I might be howling like a banshee, but I can hear the sizzle of every vile vial of cough elixir shattering on the floor. With another tug, I'm back at the cleaning aisle (though it is now looking anything but clean), dangling down from the banner, holding it as tightly as I can.

As a crowd of magic folk mutter and gasp, Bruno raises his wand. "Let the commotion stop with a steady drop. Take the firt to the ground so you'll be unwound."

The banner goes limp. I howl and grip it harder, trying to swing my leg back toward the ladder. Carefully, the banner descends to the floor. I take a deep breath and look around at the crowd. An old man attempts a slow clap, but no one joins in. They're too shocked by what they've seen.

"Thanks," I manage, though I know that Bruno charmed the banner to wrap around me and then busted half the jars with his own wand.

"It's nothing for someone with superior magical powers. Just a few incantations," he says with a smirk.

"Oh my Merlin. These antique wooden floors will be stained forever. I don't know what that firt thinks he's trying to pull off," a clerk complains.

"Good point," Benny smirks. "I do find it pathetic that a firt with so little power could cause so much damage."

My grandma says nothing through the rest of the grocery trip. If the constant gawking is getting to her, there's no way for me to tell. She tosses some morning dew and dehydrated horehound into her satchel and heads to the front of the store. One-by-one, the cashiers wave their wands in the hopes that their hovering lanterns will be off by the time we reach the cash register.

The second cashier eyes her floating lantern nervously. The fire is fading too slowly. Way too slowly. She sighs. Yep, she's dealt with Grandma Drackenberger before.

"Did you see the cleaning aisle? You're lucky we didn't make you pay for damages," the cashier growls.

"We're lucky?" my grandma says incredulously. "You're lucky we didn't sue, what with your wild banners. Get your charms under control."

As a punitive measure, my grandma starts counting out her coins as slowly as possible. Just for fun, she argues about the price of kale and demands a free jar of pixie guano for the "emotional distress" that her grandson experienced. The cashier relents and even tosses in a pack of dragon cooling breath mints just to get rid of us.

"See, that wasn't so bad," my grandma says as we step out into the flurry of Dusty Rhode Rode Road. My grandma walks up to the row of brooms, grabs the Zoom Broom 756.2 and begins sweeping away at the sidewalk. She turns to me and shrugs. "We forgot the trash-compacting bags."

"Sorry."

"No big whoop," she says sweeping away with the fanciest of travel brooms.

Bruno bursts out the door. "That lady is trying to steal my broom." Nobody notices, so he runs toward my grandma.

He shakes his fist. "Hey lady, that's my broom!"

"It can't be your broom," she says, pushing the dirt out onto the cobblestone streets. She pushes the broom into a puddle of mud. Bruno howls.

"Get your wrinkly old hands off my broom!" Bruno shouts.

"This can't be your broom. You're too young to be riding a broom," she says.

A police witch saunters up to us. "Is this young wizard bothering you?" she asks.

"Officer, she stole my broom and now she's sweeping with it. And she's ruining it."

"How old are you?" the police witch asks.

"Thirteen," he says.

"And this is your broom?"

Bruno nods. "This crazy old bag stole it from me. You can ask anyone around the village. I was flying it all morning. It's my broom."

The officer rolls out a parchment and pulls a quill out of her hair. "Underage flying is a serious offense. You can ride supervised and ride in the academy, but not in the village."

His face drops as he reads the ticket. "B-b-but I'll be at the academy. I can't . . ."

"It will take quite awhile to get back, then. Oh, and when you show up to your court date, I recommend you find a better transportation method than a broom."

As the officer walks away, my grandma smiles at Bruno. "By the way kid, if you're going to spit from atop a broom, try and improve your aim."

FOURTEEN
THE ROBOT FAIR

Sarah meets me outside the school. "You're late."

"I'm sorry. My grandma . . ."

"Talking won't make you any earlier," she says, walking me through the school gate.

The sign claims it's a Robotics Fair, but it turns out to be far from that. I'm hoping for flying robots handing balloons to kids. It would be packed with robotic rides and carnival food served by tiny robots with chain-link aprons. They'd serve bacon-wrapped circuit boards and other robot fare for the robot fair.

"This doesn't look like a fair to me," I point out. "It's not festive or anything."

"It's less like a fair and more like a competition," Sarah says. "And if you care at all about winning, you'll hurry up."

Phil meets us at the gymnasium door. "Sarah, just remember that no matter what happens, you can't pull out your wand," he says.

"You don't need to lecture me on that," she snaps.

"I'm just saying. People saw the video. It had thousands of views."

"Did anyone say it was magic?"

"Not really," he admits.

"Then there's nothing to worry about," she snaps. "They didn't see *me* do anything."

"Sorry," he mutters. "I just thought you might make sure your wand is put away."

"Oh, speaking of wands," she reaches into her satchel and pulls out a gold-colored box with a tag from Wanda's Wand Em*power*ium.

"For me?" he asks.

"It better be, because I sure can't use it," I point out.

Phil slips the fully wrapped gift into his backpack. "I'll open it later if that's okay."

"Have you done any more magic?" I ask.

He shakes his head. "I didn't have a wand. Besides, I've been focused on this competition."

"Do you think we stand a chance?" I ask as we walk into the gymnasium and head toward our robot.

"We have a flying dragon robot. I think are chances are pretty high," Sarah says.

Phil shakes his head. "You haven't met the Victors. They win every year. And, yes, each one of them is named Victor. Everyone knows their parents do all the work for them," Phil says.

I can see the look in his eyes. It's the same look I had the day of the Ceremony; the look of a kid who is trying not to hope, but is still hoping nonetheless.

"I think we can take them on," I whisper as we approach our robot. I glance at the Victors. Their robot is slick, but it's also small.

"I know what you're thinking," Phil says. "But you can't underestimate them. They always win. Always."

"I'm going to scout the course," Sarah says. "I should have been doing this an hour ago, but *somebody* couldn't wake up on time."

One of the Victors notices me staring and punches his fist. Yep, these guys are serious.

"I should probably go with her," Phil says. "You can talk to the judges, right?"

"Um, I . . ." It's too late. He scurries off.

"I, uh, I guess I can," I mumble.

CHAPTER FOURTEEN

A judge waddles up to the table and glares at me. He's wearing a shirt that reads, "Your Linux isn't dead. It's just Terminal." I have no idea what that means.

"So how long did it take you to build it?" the man points to me.

"I . . . uh . . . it was three days I guess."

"Sure it was," he smirks. "And the Pyramids were built in a week." I'm too afraid to tell him that they really were built in a week by some of the world's best wizards.

"I mean, I've been making these my whole life. They just never really worked before."

The judge flips out what looks like a super-thin computer and taps on the screen.

"So, do you see a practical use for it?" the judge asks.

"Sure. It's perfect for families that are allergic to real dragons," I say.

He chuckles. "Okay, but really, what is the function of a robodragon?"

I shrug my shoulders and try to imagine Fran Pi doing something useful. Maybe reaching a hard place?

"I was thinking rescue operations in hard to reach places. Especially icy places."

"Interesting," he mumbles, tapping away at the screen. He leaves with an awkward wave.

A tall black-haired man approaches me with a handshake. "I'm Burt. Can we talk?"

"Sure," I say, though I'm nervous the moment he ushers me away from the table. I can't imagine what Sarah would say about leaving our table unattended.

"Actually, I should probably stay with our robot," I tell him. However, he waves his hand defiantly and lowers his voice to a near-whisper, "I'm Phil's dad. I just wanted to thank you for letting him tag along."

"Actually, Sarah and I are the ones tagging along."

"I know Phil well enough to realize that he's not able to put something like that together."

"It was an equal partnership," I point out.

He shakes his head. "Well, it's nice to see him finally making some friends."

"I'm sure he has friends."

"Phil?" He chortles. "He tries. You have to give it to him. He tries. Anyway, I also wanted to invite you to join me for a bit of project. We've been looking for a design wizard." I straighten up at the term wizard.

"It's an expression," he says with a grin. "Then again, so is three x minus twelve."

"Okay."

"That was a math joke," he adds. "Anyway, I'll be rooting for you guys. I might have to leave a little early, though. Looks like you've got another judge," he says, pointing to the table.

A scowling woman meets me with crossed arms. Her face looks as tight as the bun on the back of her head.

"Sorry, ma'am."

"I don't like waiting," she says. Pointing at Fran Pi, she continues, "So, this looks like a cute toy. Can you tell me why it's anything more than that?"

"Well, it can save dead people," I say.

"I find that hard to believe. If a person is dead, then he or she hardly needs saving."

"But see if a person is stuck, the dragon can swoop down and . . ."

"Wouldn't one use a helicopter instead?" she asks.

"I guess so," I say, having no idea what a helicopter is.

"What kinds of voice recognition software do you use?"

"I don't think it has that," I say.

"And what about the climbing capabilities?"

"Well, it flies, actually. So it doesn't need . . ."

"Can it be controlled remotely?"

"Yeah . . ." I lie.

"Okay, show me how that works, then."

"I'm a . . . I'm not really sure . . ." I stammer. I can feel the blood rushing to my head. I take a deep breath and wipe the sweat from my forehead.

"Go on. Let's see it fly," she says tapping a pencil on her clipboard.

"I'm not really the one who controls it. I just kind-of helped on the design," I admit.

"Well, this looks like a nice novelty robot, but the other judges are right. It's all form and no function. I need to *see* what it's capable of accomplishing. Unless that's too much to ask of you."

"Just let me get Sarah."

She shakes her head. "Were you listening when I said that I don't like waiting?"

I gulp. "Okay, I can do it. Just watch." I step up to the computer and type "fly." Nothing happens. I type, "go ahead and fly now" and again nothing happens.

The judge taps her foot on the gym floor.

"I can do it," I say. Right as she walks away, I notice a slip of paper. I type in the code, complete with the special semi-colons that Sarah showed me yesterday. Suddenly, the dragon is flittering around, circling the woman with the clipboard. I type another set of instructions and the dragon is twirling around, zooming up toward the ceiling.

Where did she put the landing instructions? I run my finger through the code. There's nothing on it about landing. I look up, right as the dragon is inching toward a metal rafter. Hunting for each letter, my shaking finger types the "power down" instructions. Fran Pi tumbles down.

At the corner of my eye, I notice Sarah puling out her wand. She screams, "Stop the velocity with all due ferocity, all stands still to stop the atrocity."

I sprint forward and I tumble over a table. It folds out from under me. Papers are flying everywhere. My face is inches from a robot.

"What's your problem?" a kid yells.

"It's sabotage," another complains. "He's trying to take out our robot."

"I'm sorry," I mutter. Looking up, I recognize the team. It's the Victors. I wait for them to pounce on me, but instead they stare at the dragon. Everyone in the gym is staring.

"How is she doing that?" someone mumbles.

"It's not flying. It's floating. The wings. It's like they're not even moving," another Victor says.

All around, people are pulling out their phones, capturing the moment with motion pictures. Captured. That's exactly what it is. We're caught.

The judge runs toward me. "A hover craft. Impressive indeed. I thought you said it didn't have voice command?"

I shrug. "We were saving that for later."

"What kind of a device is she using?"

"A wand . . . er . . . um . . ."

"Yes, a wireless wand. Interesting term, but it makes sense. I'm amazed by the hovering abilities," she says, while the dragon floats down toward the ground.

I scurry away from the table and approach Sarah. A large crowd gathers around, hammering her with technical questions.

"I need to talk to my teammate," she says, walking me toward the exit.

"What are you doing?"

"Fixing your mistake," she says with a grin. "I don't blame you. I should have been the one working the controls."

"You could have been seen," I point out.

"I was seen," she whispers. "But no one's going to think it was magic."

"Why didn't you just let the dragon drop?"

"Really? Of anyone, I thought you would get it. He's got an empty trophy shelf and he's been doing this contest for years. We're winning this thing no matter what."

I nod. She's right. In this moment, it becomes more than just a robotics contest. It's about empty banners and empty shelves and doing something no one thinks you can accomplish.

Even with the seemingly soft landing, I still spend the thirty-minute break fixing screws and joints on the dragon. Sarah shows me the screen. It turns out she controls it through a "program" with fancy buttons instead of hand typing in directions. When I try to touch the screen, she slaps my hand away.

"You're not touching it. Whatever happens, you're not touching it."

Together we carry Fran Pi to the starting area.

Sarah smiles. "I think she'll capture the flags pretty easily. I looked at the course and I really don't think they considered robotic dragons. Clearly we have the advantage," Sarah points out.

As we place our robot on the starting line, the coordinator taps on the microphone. "Attention. We have a last minute change in order to test the adaptability of our contestants. There will now be a flag that the robots will have to retrieve inside of the bucket."

Phil shakes head. "That's Victor's dad," he whispers.

"Which Victor?"

"The mean one." He might as well say, "all the Victors."

"You think it was aimed at us?" I ask.

Sarah nods. "Fran'll be fried if she dives in."

I exhale and stare at the breath in front of my face. Even if it's late morning, it still feels freezing. I turn around and notice the crowd huddling around in their jackets and breathing into their mugs of coffee. A man in a knit hat points at our dragon.

"You seem nervous," Sarah says.

"Aren't you?" I ask.

"Not right now. I'm more nervous about tonight," she says.

"What's tonight?" I ask.

She smiles. "Right, it's our little secret. Let's just see how this dragon flies."

"Is that Mr. Oglesby?" I point. Sarah turns around, but the man is gone.

"Take your marks," the coordinator says. "Five, four, three, two . . ." An earsplitting buzzer announces the start. Our dragon hops along awkwardly. She's a solid ten feet behind the last place robot.

"Is she going to fly?" Phil asks.

"Wait for it. Wait for it. Now," Sarah says. Fran Pi's wings flap awkwardly, but she's airborne. Gaining speed, she darts through the pillars and zips around the hallways, passing her competition along the way. As the robots struggle to climb the incline, Fran Pi soars above the wall and snags the first flag. Next, she swoops down and snatches the basketball to add additional points.

Sarah squints at the video camera on the screen, waiting until Fran is inches away to drop it down the rim. She maneuvers the claws and the ball swooshes through the hoop.

The other robots are still maneuvering around the incline, with several falling down backward, stuck in a robotic paralysis. Sarah taps on the screen, carefully maneuvering the robot through the low silver hoops, where Fran promptly snatches two more flags. Then it's on to the bucket of water.

I exhale and stare at my breath as the dragon hovers above the bucket.

"What do we do?" Sarah asks.

"It's only a few inches deep."

"We didn't protect any of the bottom wires, though," Sarah points out.

"Can we knock the bucket over?"

"It's too risky," Phil says. "Plus, we'll lose points."

"Well sometimes you have to take risks," Sarah points out. "Do you want to win this thing or not?"

I take another deep breath and stare at the steam in front of my face.

"That's it. Steam. How hot is her fire?"

"It's really hot," Phil says.

"So, we make the water evaporate."

"That might work," Sarah says, tightening the strings on her hoodie. She taps away at the screen and all at once the dragon hovers above the bucket and sprays a huge stream of fire.

The crowd gasps. We wait for what seems like ages.

"What can you see?" Phil asks.

"The camera is too steamy," Sarah says. "But it might be enough." She pulls the dragon back up and waits for the steam to clear.

I study the screen. It's made hardly any difference. "Just do it again," Phil says. "It can't take too much more."

We wait while the dragon spews the fire again. Steam floats up. The bucket starts turning black. Ten minutes pass by and still the steam rises. The other robots are tossing the balls into the hoop. The race is getting closer. Way too close.

The area looks like a sauna. She has to be within a few minutes of snagging the flag.

"Could we skip this part?" Phil asks.

"Be patient," Sarah says.

Finally, the robot soars up. Sarah waits while the Victors' robot scales a wall and barrels toward the bucket.

With pursed lips, she maneuvers the robot toward a freefall. In one movement, it snatches the tiny, wet flag and floats upward. The crowd screams. With so many robots now out of commission, the remaining teams are cheering us on. Sarah taps on the screen again and aims the dragon toward the finish line. Suddenly, a boy from the Victors runs toward us. He trips on my shoe and pulls Sarah down with him.

Without thinking, Phil pulls the wand out of Sarah's sweatshirt pocket and aims it at the dragon. "Let this be clear. Freeze in midair." I gaze into the camera. Suddenly frost is forming around the wings. A frost charm. It's a rookie mistake.

I press the fire button on the program. To my surprise, it works. The hovering dragon begins thawing out. Still, the Victors' robot is barreling toward the finish line.

"That was on purpose!" Sarah yells, but the boy who ran into her is faking a broken arm.

"I'm sorry. I just slipped," he lies. He turns to me and whispers, "That's for the table trick." I close my eyes and take a deep breath.

"Tap out of the window," Phil says, still aiming his wand at Fran Pi.

"There isn't a window," I shoot back.

"Just click on the red circle and then control the rest." Phil is right. I tap on the circle and suddenly the controls are in front of me. I hold down the acceleration button and aim the dragon's face toward the finish line. It isn't graceful. She looks like a drunken hawk, but she is gaining speed.

The crowd rushes toward the finish line. I click on the "boost" button. The wings flap faster than I've ever seen. Smoke streams behind her as she zips past the Victors' robot and then sputters to a stop, falling inches from the finish line.

Sarah gasps.

I shake my head. "I . . . uh . . . I thought it would work . . ."

"We never tested it," she points out, still writhing in pain.

I continue pressing the acceleration button. The wings flap awkwardly. The Victors' robot sprints forward as our dragon hobbles over the finish line.

It's too close to call.

"The judges will be examining the video," a woman announces.

We huddle together and Phil shakes his head. "I can't believe I did that. I mean . . . if people find out . . ."

"For doing magic?" Sarah asks.

He nods.

"They can't kick you out of the enchanted world if you're not already in it," she points out.

"Really?"

"Yeah, it's like a loophole. You can say that you never knew any better. So, you're good."

He takes a deep breath. "Was it cheating?" he asks.

I laugh. "Really? They sent a person to crash into us. I think we're okay on the ethical quandary of using magic at the last minute."

"Okay," he says.

We gather together in the gymnasium and wait through a series of speeches on science and technology.

"Where's my dad?" Phil asks.

"He said he might have to leave early," I point out.

"Yeah, that sounds like him."

After going through honorable mentions and announcing the third place contestant, the lead judge stares out at the crowd. "The top two winners will move on to the state championship this Saturday. I think it's clear who the final two teams are, so we will announce the first place finisher followed by the second. And here to announce the winner is Dr. Benjamin Barzoinkonium."

A short man walks up the podium. "Ah, what you saw today was wonderful. Indeed, I would even call it *magical.*" Instantly, I recognize the voice. It's Benny. But he's freshly shaved and isn't wearing a hat.

"For the first time in three years, we have a new team of winners . . ." The crowd screams so loudly I can't hear the rest of his words. Phil and I both stand up in a daze, while Sarah jumps toward the stage.

Phil and I are beaming. It's the first time we've ever won anything.

1ST PLACE

212

FIFTEEN
FILBERT

"Wendell Darrell Drackenberger!"

I spin around to see my mom bolting across the graveyard. She scoops me up and holds me as tightly as her petite arms will allow.

"I'm fine," I mutter.

"Where have you been?" she asks.

"I went to the library."

"I searched through the rubble and didn't see you. When did you escape?"

I stare at the ground. She hugs me harder. "Greg said he saw you running toward Smells Like Bundt, but when I looked around no one was there," she adds.

"It's a blur, mom. I'm just glad to see you." What is she talking about? What happened?

Her face is drenched in tears and she holds my hand like I'm a toddler.

Smoke billows from Noah's Arcade as we step out of the Sedentary Cemetery and head toward the Town Tetrahedron. The ground is soaked with wet ash and the clouds are still hanging around, just in case.

The toys are motionless at Wallybombers. Stray images of screaming kids float from the freshly pressed papers flying out of the *Wizarding Word* and into the village homes. Nerdy Nick's Library is nothing but rubble and Noah's Arcade is now reduced to scrap wood and brick.

"Twelve children are in critical condition," a phonograph breaks the silence.

"Looks like your dad will be working late. They need every nurse they can get," my mom says, pointing to signage at Scary Hairy Gary the Apothecary. Even the typically raucous crowd at the Gnome Home stares at the ground as they puff on their pipes.

As we reach the castle, my mom points out the new doorknob. "I had it installed this morning. I still think you're magical. I just thought this might be a little more convenient until your abilities kick in."

I lock myself in my room and cuddle up to Ash. For the first time all week, I'm feeling guilty about lying. I wanted to do something different. Something I was good at. I did. We won the trophy. However, now I'm feeling trapped.

Nobody says anything at dinner. We push around our food, unable to comprehend what just happened.

I spend the night wrestling with the sheets, bombarded by images of the smoke and the screaming and the village up in flames.

I wake up the next morning confused by the whole situation. If Benny was truly running the Misfits, why was he at the Robotics Fair? And why did Phil's dad (What was his name, Burt?) talk about wizards? Why doesn't Phil go by Burt if he's named after his dad?

"Phil. Burt," I mumble. "No way. It can't be." I jump up, startling Ash. Thankfully, she lets out nothing more than a warm yawn. After putting on my robe and packing up a pair of jeans and a hoodie, my mom greets me at the kitchen table.

"I made cinnamon rolls," she says.

"Don't you have to be at work?" I ask.

"Oh, honey, we're all taking the day off. If the Misfits are attacking, we'd better wait for the authorities to handle it before we open shop again."

"Your store wasn't even attacked."

"Yeah, but they're still pretty nervous about it. Besides, my boss thinks the Misfits were trying to buy maps. So, I'll be staying home today."

"How long will you be here?"

"It could be days."

Days? No way. I need to see Sarah. She needs to know about Filbert.

My mom smiles, "But you know, I was thinking that we could have fun together. You could show me some of those Bored Games you got from Benny. I'd rather you play with those than the smelly markers."

That's it. Benny's markers.

"Actually, mom, I'm not feeling too great this morning."

"Is it the smoke? You know, I did a charm when I first saw you and I never smelled any smoke on you the whole evening."

"No, it's my stomach. I think it's last night's dinner," I lie. "It's actually made me kind-of gassy. Do you mind if I stay in the guest room while I let it rip?"

She grimaces as I walk back to the room (a converted robe closet) and do the best fake farts I can manage. Big blubbering ones on my inner elbow.

"Are you feeling okay?" my mom asks.

"I wouldn't come in if I were you," I warn her. As she mutters the door-opening charm, I uncap Benny's markers. Instantly, the room reeks of flatulence. Even I can't hold back a cough.

"I told you mom. I should probably just stay in here all day if that's all right with you."

"I suppose it's not smart to have the dragon with you."

"Not unless we want it to explode," I tell her.

"Did you ever clip her wings?" she asks, shutting the door.

"I will today," I respond.

"Well, I don't want her flying away," my mom warns. I uncap three more markers, hold my breath and crack the door open. It feels like an eternity as she meanders around the kitchen muttering spells.

Finally, she decides to head upstairs. I dart toward the door.

"Where are you going?" my sister whispers.

"Um, you can't tell anyone that I'm leaving," I say.

"You want me to lie?" she asks.

"It's for a good cause," I say, though I'm feeling guilty that my little sister is now in on the dishonesty.

"I don't like lying," she whispers.

"Please. I'm going to try and stop the Misfits."

"Okay," she says reluctantly. I tap her on the forehead; something she clearly hates, given the death stare she gives me in return. Then I take off in a full sprint, across the eerily silent Town Tetrahedron and into the Sedentary Cemetery.

Instead of entering the catacombs, I jog around the graveyard until I reach Sarah's shack. It's a rickety place with missing boards held up by nothing more than a charm. I reach for the doorknob. Of course not. Nobody around here has a doorknob. So, I knock.

"Who's there?" a man yells.

"Um, is Sarah there?"

"You didn't answer my question. Who's there?"

"This is Wendell," I respond.

"Oh, Wendell. Yes, I've heard about you. You're the kid who left my daughter to fend for herself in a den of zombies last night."

That was last night? How could I have forgotten that?

"Is she okay?"

"She's alive, if that's what you mean," her dad responds.

"Look, sir . . ."

"Don't call me sir. I'm not a knight," he snarls.

"Well, I didn't mean to leave her alone."

"It's not about what you meant. It's what you did. Now if you had any idea of what's good for you, you'd leave right now."

"Harold?" a voice calls out from the back of the house. "Is that Wendell?"

"It sure is."

"Well, let him in already," she says.

"I suppose you have a plan, then? The boy can't do magic and we can't open doors. Unless you've forgotten that we're ghosts."

"Post-living," she corrects him.

"Post-living my behind. We're ghosts. Ghouls. Specters. Just don't say that we're post-living."

"Wendell, dear," she calls out. "Just crawl through the window, okay?"

I step up to the tiny window and lift it up. Instantaneously, it expands into a bay window. I step inside and tumble to the ground.

"I'd give you a hand, but it would do no good," a woman says.

"No good? He's the no-good . . ." her father begins.

"Would you like some hot chocolate? You'll have to get it yourself, seeing as how I can't pick anything up." I approach the cauldron and ladle the hot chocolate (more like lukewarm chocolate) into a mug.

"So, what did you need to tell Sarah?" her dad demands.

"I should probably go."

"Nonsense. He's just in a bad mood," she says. "He tends to get a little overprotective about our daughter."

"I told her to stay out of the DUMP," the man says.

"I think we saw Filbert. I think he's alive."

Both of them stop and cross their arms. "He was watching our robotics project. Um, he kind-of asked me if I wanted to work for him."

"That's impossible," Mrs. Bellum says. "He died when his jet crashed. Benny saw the whole thing."

"What's a jet?" I ask.

"It's nothing . . . uh . . . it's like a . . . like a metal dragon thing, but it floats more smoothly," Mrs. Bellum says, pointing to a newspaper.

"Isn't it expensive?" I say, taking a sip from my lukewarm chocolate.

"The Misfits have money. Between donations and smuggling, they've got the money," Sarah's mom explains.

"Do you know where Sarah is?" I ask.

Her dad hovers around my face. "She's in the DUMP looking for you. She's lucky she's alive."

Without so much as a goodbye, I jump through the window, race to the catacombs and sneak in. It's harder this time, with more zombies patrolling the corridors. However, given their slow speed and all-too-obvious torches, I maneuver around the maze and exit into the park.

"Wendell!" Phil shouts from the swing set. His face is red. It looks like he's been crying.

I approach him reluctantly.

"What's your problem?" he asks.

"I'm just late is all. I have a lot of things going on right now. Have you seen Sarah?"

He shakes his head. "But we only have a few days and we need to figure out how to make it work under water."

"I don't know if I can make it today."

"Oh, I see," he says, sitting back down on the swing. "Is it something I did?"

"No, I'm kind-of grounded."

"Well, I can work on it myself, I guess."

"Hey, can I ask you something? Is Phil your real name?"

"Kind-of," he says. "It's actually Filbert."

"Filbert?"

"I know. It sucks, but it's a family name."

"You were named after your dad?"

"Of course I was named *after* my dad. I couldn't be named *before* him," he says, trying to muster a grin. I can't even crack a smile. Should I tell him or keep this to myself?

"What's wrong?"

"Nothing. Um, have you told him about your abilities?"

"To do magic?" he asks.

"Yeah." Oh my Merlin. I'm talking to Filbert's son. My heart is picking up speed and my mind can't keep up the pace.

"There hasn't been time," he says. "My dad suddenly got busy over the last few weeks. He's stood me up twice and he even left our competition early."

"Do you remember the story of Filbert the Firt?" I lean in to whisper. "Well that was your dad."

We stand there staring for a silent eternity. He shakes his head. "It's not true."

"There was an attack yesterday and I think he was behind it," I say, pacing in front of the swings.

"He's not like that." His face is pale. Blotches are forming on his neck.

"The facts add up. I know you don't want to admit it, but that's the truth." He looks up from the swing and narrows his eyes at me.

"I think I get it now. Is that why Sarah isn't here? You think my dad is a murderer and now you don't want to work with me."

"Look! It's not like that. I promise. We need to find Sarah. You can come with me. But I'm telling you, it's guarded by zombies."

"Zombies? Is it really? Or are you just saying that because you know I'll be afraid?"

"Uh, it . . . it's not like that," I stammer.

"No, it is! It's exactly like that. You guys don't want to work with me. Go ahead. Leave. But you're wrong about me and you're wrong about my dad."

Somehow it feels worse to hear the dejected tone of his voice; worse than if he'd just yelled and stormed off.

"You can come with me. We'll look for her together. However, I'm telling you that it's guarded by . . ."

Phil spins himself into a knot. The chains clank together until it's as tight as possible. Then, he lets go. The swing whirls around, but before it stops, he takes off at a sprint.

I kick at a rock on the way back to the shrubs. I want to help him with the robot. I want to win the competition. However, if Sarah is working on a stopping the Misfits, I want to be a part of that, too.

I close my eyes and gulp. As I step through the tunnel, a sudden jolt shoots up my back.

"Stop!"

CHAPTER FIFTEEN

I hold my hands above my head. My heart is racing. This day is turning out to be nothing like I had imagined.

"Mr. Dragonbooger," a man says.

"Um . . . i . . . i . . . it's Drackenberger, sir," I barely get out.

"You're coming with us," he says, aiming his wand at my throat.

Two police wizards aim their wands at me as well. I follow them past the staring zombies and through the maze of tunnels.

"Don't say anything," a tiny voice whispers in my ear. I turn around to see a less intoxicated Dr. Larry Faerie the Fairy perched on my shoulder.

"This way Wendell," the wizard says, waving his wand at a rusted metal door. My heart is racing.

"It's not illegal to go to the DUMP," I blurt out.

The man shakes his head and waves me inside. "This way," the officer says, leading me through another corridor, where I see a map with the Misfits targets.

"Are you part of the Misfits?" I ask.

"We're wondering the same about you," a man says. As he steps forward I recognize the bald head and gloomy eyes of Mr. Oglesby.

"Why are you with us, Mr. Oglesby?"

"Just walk inside," he instructs.

The door pops open. A woman greets me with an overly perky grin. She looks like an ostrich with an old-lady head. Her voice is a squawk and her robes flutter around her, but her neck is skinny. I want to stare at her, but I keep my eyes on my own feet.

"From this point on, we'll ask the questions," she says.

"Take a seat," Mr. Oglesby says. Inside is a long rectangular table. I swallow hard and pull up the only remaining empty chair.

Sarah glares at me from across the table. I'm pretty sure she's not doing a shrinking spell, but I feel two inches tall right now.

"Why am I here?"

"From this point on we will be asking questions. I knew you were a firt, but I had no idea it affected your ability to comprehend basic instructions," the woman says with a smirk.

Mr. Oglesby leans across the table. "Do you know Sarah Bellum?"

I nod.

"Did you see Miss Bellum perform magic in the DUMP?"

I remain silent.

"You stand accused of no crimes. Entering the DUMP is unwise, but it isn't criminal. Failing to cooperate, however . . ."

I continue to remain silent.

Ostrich Lady steps up to the wall, taps her wand and waits for an image to float off of an empty frame.

"Thanks to Agent Oglesby, we have video. Our entire way of life has been compromised," she says.

"It wasn't on purpose. We just wanted to win. I screwed it up and she landed it for me."

"Excuse me?"

"Yeah, at the contest," I rush on. "I was the one who ran into the Victors. She was actually trying to help out."

"This is worse than we thought. That dragon was yours?" the woman asks.

"Um, no. I was . . . no . . ."

"I told you that their dragon was enchanted," Mr. Oglesby says. He turns to me. "And to think that I was going to allow you to work on the side of law enforcement."

"You don't understand . . ."

"Don't use that tone with us," Ostrich Lady says.

"Sarah was doing everything right. She was trying to help."

I glance at Sarah and realize too late that she's shaking her head at me behind their backs.

"Do you recognize these keys?" Mr. Oglesby asks. They echo as he drops them on the table.

"I don't know where these are from," I lie, staring at the keys from Charles the Brain-Intolerant Zombie.

"I think he was acting alone," the woman says. Turning to me, she says, "You may go. It seems clear that you were the victim of someone else's scheme."

I look back at Sarah, face buried in her palms. Mr. Oglesby stands up and aims his wand at the door. My stomach sinks. Sarah's taking the fall because I was too scared to tell the truth.

SIXTEEN
THE CONFESSION

I wake up the next morning cold and alone. Even my pet dragon doesn't want to be around me. I trudge down to the dark kitchen and tap away at our mobile message typewriter.

The lamp beside me begins to burn. Must be a clever new movement sensor charm. Greg is like that. He can fix anything with a spell.

I tell everything: the stolen keys, the zombies and the magical part I used on the robot dragon. I tap the send button and watch the paper transform into a crane. It zips around the kitchen while I attempt to open the window

"Looking for something?" Greg asks, crumpling the mobile message in his hand.

"The police need to know the truth," I say.

"No, they don't."

"That's not fair to Sarah," I point out.

"Ever thought of what you've done to the family? Sarah's picture is on every paper. They're talking about her on all the phonographs. You want that kind of attention on our family?"

"I don't, but . . ."

"Just tell me, Wendell, are you doing this for Sarah or are you doing this to clear your conscience?"

"It's the right thing to do," I point out.

"Since when did you start thinking about the right thing to do? You'll do your confession and then you'll take off to the DUMP and we'll be left with the aftermath."

"I didn't choose to be a firt."

"No, you didn't. But you chose to lie. You chose to sneak off. Why couldn't you have just sat at home like a normal firt?"

"Fine, I won't say anything," I lie. I spend the next few hours shivering in my bedroom. Maybe Greg's right. Maybe I should have stayed in my room like a normal firt and kept to myself.

My mom barges into my room. "Have you seen Ash Lee?"

I shake my head.

"You clipped her wings, didn't you?"

"Yeah," I lie. Again.

She sighs. "Then she'll come back. Probably got distracted doing her business. Are you feeling better?"

I nod.

"Because I was thinking that it's not fair to ask you to stay here the whole time." She hands me a stack of coins.

"Thanks."

"You didn't know that Sarah girl did you?"

"Um, no. Not really. I mean she was a classmate, but not a close friend."

"I knew you were better than that. You know, you've handled things well. You could have gone to the DUMP and instead you went to the library," she says with a smile. "And I still think you'll do something magical one of these days."

Minutes after she leaves, I head out toward the Town Tetrahedron. For all the repair magic they've mustered, the buildings are still charred up. The accordions sound like a herd of wheezing donkeys. The guitars are tinny and weak. Even the banjos sound sad. Really, how do you make a banjo sound sad?

I consider buying a hot butterscotch from the Gnome Home, but I don't want to be around anyone. Without realizing it, my feet carry me to the police precinct. I stand on the steps debating whether to walk away or go inside. I remember Greg's words. Maybe it's best to stay silent and let it settle.

But Sarah's face, despondent and hidden in her hands, settles in my mind. I can't decide, so I don't. I walk around the block, bumping into a banjo and nearly knocking down a witch crying by Scary Hairy Gary's Apothecary.

Things would be fine if I did nothing at all. Sarah would probably get off easy, since it's her first offense. I could follow Greg's advice and stay out of trouble. However, I'd be hiding. Forever. If I tell the truth, it's out there. Yeah, and everyone will hate me . . . for a while. Over time, though, they'd get over it. Wouldn't they?

My mind cycles through every scenario until I round the final corner and step back to the door at the police precincts.

I step inside.

"Can I help you?" a receptionist asks.

"Yeah, I need to explain something."

"Has there been another attack?"

I shake my head. "I just need to explain a few things."

The same perky woman from yesterday walks me back to a room with two chairs and a tree with floating candles charmed to change colors with the mood of the room. The bright red fades into a dark blue.

My uncle walks in. "What're you doing here? Do you have some information that might help us with Sarah's trial?"

"I do."

"Go on," he scowls. I'm shaking. I can't speak. A few times I sputter out some uhs and ums, but the words won't come out.

"I can do a heating charm if you're cold," he offers.

"I took the keys to the zombies. I wanted to find the Misfits."

He shakes his head and pulls out a quill. "Wendell, you should keep this quiet."

I shake my head.

"Think about what you'll do to the family name. Just lay low and let it play out on its own."

"I also know that Filbert is alive," I point out.

"Nonsense. He died years ago," my uncle says.

Mr. Oglesby barges through the door. "I'll take over at this point."

"You're sure that Filbert is alive?" he asks.

"Yeah, I met him."

"And you said nothing about it?"

I shrug my shoulders.

"Is this all you needed to tell me?"

I'm tempted to leave it here. I'm already in enough trouble. "Actually, you probably heard about the robot dragon. It had enchanted parts. I kind-of took them from our village and used them in the DUMP."

He pulls off his spectacles and rubs his eyes. "This is . . . this is serious."

"I know," is all I can manage to say.

"You stole the keys from the zombies and you used enchanted devices in the DUMP?"

"I thought we could find where the Misfits were hiding. I knew that Filbert was alive."

He walks me through an underground tunnel that leads to a jail cell. It's awful in those four walls, not knowing what's happening outside. I worry about how my family is going to take all of this. My mom's heart is going to break. I can only imagine my dad's cold and un-dramatic wrath. That is the worst; anger so deep that it cannot be expressed.

Mildred always seems to have connections and knowledge. Maybe I should go to her. She can hide me somewhere until this all blows over.

What about that prophesy? If by doing something great, she meant that I would make a great mess of things then maybe her prophecy was right. I think about her losing her fortune-tellers license. She bounced back. Maybe there's hope for me. I could bounce back . . . eventually.

Suddenly I realize that I've been so focused on my own humiliation that I never stopped to think about anyone else's experiences. Will my little sister be picked on at school? Will this ruin her future? Will my parents face retaliation at work?

It strikes me that there's nothing wrong with being a firt. It's something I'm stuck with. However, I chose to lie. Over and over again, I lied. I chose to sneak to the DUMP and it wasn't just to help the village. I wanted to win the contest.

Steps echo in the jail corridor.

"He'll probably be barred from doing magic. Then again, it really won't make much of a difference," the female police officer says.

My dad's face appears between the bars and I jump up. Silent tears stream down my face. I don't know what he's thinking or feeling until he gives me one of those back-pounding man-hugs.

We walk home in silence. When we reach the door, he looks into my eyes. "I wasn't embarrassed when you were a firt. I wasn't embarrassed when I found out you couldn't play schnorbitz. But this. This I'm ashamed of. You lied to us. Twice we thought you were dead when, in reality, you were doing nothing but sneaking out and lying to us. You should be ashamed."

SEVENTEEN
DEADLINE

Between the disappearance of Ash and the confession I wrote, the house feels uninhabitable. I step out into the moonlit cobblestone. I'm wishing I could step back into the last Friday and take up Benny's offer.

Maybe I still can. I mean, my parents will think I'm taking the safe route. I wouldn't *really* be lying to them. I would still be working for Benny. I'm not sure that I could do much to help, but after walking through the destruction, I want to do something – anything – to stop the Misfits before they attack the Bezaudorf again.

I get it. The village has been awful to me, but the truth is that I've been awful, too. I jeopardized the entire enchanted world in order to win a shiny piece of plastic. I told myself it was about Phil, but it was about me. It was about payback, about proving I was more than just a firt.

I march over to Benny's house and take a deep breath. This is it. I bang on the door. Nobody answers. I pound on the door again. "What do you want?" he snarls.

"It's Wendell. I want to talk to you."

The door bursts open. "Make yourself at home. Or better yet, don't make yourself too welcome."

I hold my breath and step inside.

"Finally figured out that it wasn't me?"

"Yeah, I'm sorry. I just saw some things that made me think you were one of the Misfits."

"Well, I thought you were a kid with integrity, so I suppose we were both wrong about each other," he says.

"I'm going to go. This was a bad idea," I say standing up. "But I'm sorry. I feel horrible."

He sighs. "Just sit down and let me think about it." He rubs his temple and then walks down a set of stairs into his lair. Note to self: I need to quit thinking of it as a lair or thinking about his employees as minions. He's not a villain anymore.

I sit down on a bright orange vinyl couch, expecting it to feel like a park bench. Instead, it moulds around me in a comfortable recline. Engineering really does feel like magic.

"I'm not sure there's anything we can do," he calls out from the stairs. "The attack is tomorrow and we still can't get our project to work."

"You think they'll have a jet?"

He strokes his beard (it's bizarre how fast a fully shaved gnome will grow a beard). "I think so, but I'm not one hundred percent sure. Wait a second . . . how do you know?"

"I just do," I respond. "You know, if we could get Sarah on board, we could figure out a solution. She'll want to get back at Filbert."

Looking away, he sighs. "She's pretty angry with you."

"How'd you hear about it?"

"It's a long story," he says. "Let's talk to your parents."

He follows me back to my castle and talks to my parents about a possible apprenticeship.

"Just know that you're getting a kid who lies," my dad says. "Maybe you can do better by him than I have apparently done."

My mom doesn't say a word the whole time. It's almost like they're glad that someone else will be responsible for their screw-up of a firt.

"I know exactly who I'm getting," Benny says. "That's why I figured I could whip him into shape with some hard physical labor tonight."

"I'm fine with that," my mom says. The road to the Gnome Home is still blocked off, so we have to go the long route into the Town

Tetrahedron. We cut through the backside of Spell It Correctly!, where I can hear a group of elves debating the merit of the new anti-aircraft charms.

Together, we march through the Town Tetrahedron. It's quiet for a Friday night, but that's almost worse. Every word spoken is about me. Already wizards are speculating that I'll be the next Filbert. It doesn't help to see my face floating off the newspapers, illuminated by the floating lanterns above.

It feels like eternity by the time we pass the scowling wizards outside the courthouse, circle Mr. Macnology's Site for Sight and duck under the hovering Do Not Enter tape in front of the Gnome Home.

Sarah meets me at the door. "You're late," she points out, holding a mobile message.

"I'm glad you're okay," I respond.

"Just because we're working together doesn't mean we're friends again. The zombies could have killed me. And thanks to you, I'm a full day behind."

"I'm sorry," I say. "But I thought you should know that I confessed to everything."

"It's a little late for that. Besides, you weren't the one who got me off the hook. Someone came forward and confessed."

"Did they say who it was?"

She shakes her head.

I follow her through the empty restaurant and back to Benny's office. The glorious room of a few days ago is now picked over, with parts strewn everywhere. Spechwalph hands me their initial list of plans. I'm not saying it's an awful plan, but it certainly has a troll-like feel to it.

I shake my head at the ideas.

"Ignore their plans, Wendell. I've been working on a dragon," she says. "It's the only thing that could take down a jet."

"So that's what you've been working on?"

She nods. "Yep. This is the secret project."

"Our last dragon was pretty impressive," I point out.

Use a catapult (or maybe a trebuchet) to launch poop at the Misfits. It'll be a game. We'll call it "Angry Turds."

Send them a gift unicorn packed full of angry, bloodthirsty pixies. (Attribution: we stole this idea from the Greeks*)

Shoot flaming arrows at them. Oh, wait, never mind. That was a bad idea. Those arrows will fall straight back down on us.

We're pretty sure that it's actually within the public domain.

"Yeah, but physics will be tougher. The weight changes when you scale. Even with magic, we're fighting an uphill battle against gravity. It's a basic principle of physics."

"I know that already," I snarl. She can mock me for my lack of magic, but I know a thing or two about physics.

She whips out her wand and sends a blanket flying toward the trolls. The dragon appears. It looks less like a dragon and more like a giant rusted metal bat. The holster seems too small for her and too big for Benny.

"It isn't pretty, but . . ."

"No," I smile. "It's amazing."

She rolls her eyes. "Anyway, I thought you could get to work on the flight patterns."

I pull out the smelly markers and choose the best option I can find. Soon, the room smells like fresh-cut grass as I sketch out the plans for a robot dragon.

When Sarah corrects my sketch, a troll runs in and yells, "If you were a triangle, you'd be ninety degrees, because you insist on being right all the time."

"Really? That's the best you've got?" Sarah asks.

"W . . . w . . . well, I'm tired," he says. "And I've never really liked insults."

"Try again," she says.

"How about this one? Your broom only flies left. No, wait. Wait. I can get this. Your broom can't go left because . . ."

"I have to be right all the time?" she asks.

"Yeah," he says, hanging his head in shame. Minutes later, Spechwalph and another troll come in and yell insults at us (ones I wouldn't repeat in this book) in the name of "constructive criticism." I add a troll brigade to our plan of attack.

"Good thinking," she says. Then, catching herself off guard, she adds, "it *might* work."

Sarah isn't nice, per se. However, we work out a system together. She taps away at the keyboard while I rearrange parts.

We run into a snag the moment we try creating the wings. It's not just an issue of weight. The truth is that I don't know how to make the movement happen. I adjust the bearings while she types out a new command line.

The dragon wings flap around wildly.

"Make it stop," I plead.

"I'm trying," she says, typing her magic charms into the computer.

The dragon flops around like a soapy fish, whacking Spechwalph in the gut and sending him flying into a giant vial of glowing elixir. He shakes his fist at us, but the glowing pink liquid oozes onto his clothes.

As the dragon wings slow down, Spechwalph wipes the liquid off of his face and licks his finger.

"It's nothing but cotton candy elixir," he mutters. Benny runs in right as Spechwalph shoves a handful in his mouth.

"That's optimism potion," Benny says.

"You're an idiot," Spechwalph says, guzzling the rest of the vial. "It's for growing cotton candy."

Next thing I know, Spechwalph is doing cartwheels in a song and dance number about the power of teamwork. "Gimme a T."

"Why can't we get it to work?" Sarah asks.

I shrug.

"Have I ever told you about the train that couldn't get to a top of the hill? He kept telling himself that he could and . . ."

Sarah shakes her head as Spechwalph retells every detail. She points at me. "Just do what you did last time on the small dragon," she says.

"It's not that easy," I point out.

"Let's just start out with the wing movement on the small dragon."

Spechwalph jumps in front of us. "I love dragons. They're so cute and cuddly and warm. Warmth. That's what we need in this world. Warmth."

"Can someone get him out of here?" Sarah asks. Two trolls push him into the empty restaurant.

"What did you do before?" Sarah asks.

"It wasn't me, actually," I confess.

"Are you serious?"

"Benny let me borrow a tiny dragon. Don't worry. We can still get this to work. We're really close."

"It's not going to happen, Wendell. Maybe we should get a real designer to work on this. Maybe one who actually knows a few things about magic."

Sarah looks up as Benny walks in. "Hey, you invented a robot dragon before. How do we get it to fly?"

He shrugs. "That was decades ago. I can hardly remember what I ate for dinner last night." Then picking at his teeth, he grins. "Looks like it was beef stew."

Sarah shakes her first. "I should have known."

"How would you know what I had for dinner?" he asks. As she storms off into the empty restaurant, Benny saunters over. "Wendell, we have a really important job. It could be dangerous, but it'll give you a break for a bit."

"At this point, I'll take up a job flossing dragons if it means getting away from Sarah."

"Point taken. Could you go to Sally's Smart Mart and see if you can find a book about stopping jets in midair?"

"You want me to do research?"

He nods.

"I was kind-of hoping I could do something a little more exciting."

"Exciting? There's nothing more exciting than research," he says.

The closest thing to danger I encounter is ducking under some caution tape as I dash toward Sally's Smart Mart and climb the spiraling bookcase up the tree house.

"Shop's closed," Sally says, snatching a floating candle.

"Benny sent me."

"This way," she says, walking me back to the secret DUMP room, complete with "READ" posters, just like that in all caps, without so much as a "please" attached. I find it odd that folks in a smart mart would need a sign to remind them to read.

I pour over two books about jet propulsion, but I can't seem to find any weaknesses. I can distract a pilot, but according to the book, there are jets called drones that are controlled remotely. I can mess with the weather conditions, but that won't happen without a weather wizard – and those are extremely rare. I could try and take away the jet fuel, but that seems difficult to do in the air. I can also send a flock of birds in to jam up the engine. However, that sounds cruel.

I think about Sarah and Benny in the tiny workshop. Our chances are small. That's it. We'll win with size. The solution has to be something small. Our giant dragon won't stand a chance against a drone. However, with small dragons, we just might make it.

I slam the book shut, step out the window and take the zip line down to the street.

As I approach the courthouse, a man holds out a wand. Instinctively, I stop and hold up my hands. It's Filbert. Wait, it's Filbert. He's a firt. I put my hands down.

"Wendell, if you see my son, can you give this to him? It's a quality wand. I was never able to use it."

I snatch it from his hand. Lunging forward, he picks me up by my robes. A second figure steps out. Even in the dim light, I recognize her immediately.

"Mildred!" Filbert lets go and sprints toward the graveyard. "I'm so glad you were here."

"It's not too late to help us," she says.

I shake my head. "I think you're wrong about Benny."

"I hope I am," she says with a grin. "But just in case, what can you tell me about the work you guys are doing?"

"How did you know I was working with him?"

"I saw you sneak out of the Gnome Home. Now, what kind of work is he having you do?" she asks impatiently.

"We're trying to stop the Misfits."

"So am I," she says. "I just worry that you might actually be working with the Misfits instead. He doesn't have you building aircrafts, does he?"

"Why?"

"Well, I just find it suspicious that the best engineer in Bezaudorf was kicked out by the elves and suddenly we've had attacks. I hope you're not helping the enemy."

"I need to go."

"I won't keep you," she says with a smile.

I dash back to the Gnome Home wondering if I'm wrong. What if Mildred is right? What if Benny is heading up the Misfits? What if we're actually helping the enemy?

Spechwalph meets me at the Gnome Home with a grin. "Want a hug? You look like you could use a hug."

"I don't want a hug," I say.

"How about an awkward sideways man hug?"

"No thanks."

"How about a sticker?" Spechwalph has a habit of asking little kids if they want stickers and when they say "yes" he pricks them with a thorn. However, this time he has a roll of dancing pegasae stickers that he stuffs in my pocket.

"I'm good."

"You are good," he says, punching me in the arm. "You're gooder than good. You're the Goodinator. You'll do terrific, kiddo."

Sarah meets me in the backroom. "We've made some great progress on the dragon," she says rubbing her eyes.

"Yeah, I had a thought about that. What if we don't need to go big?"

"I'm not seeing your point," Sarah says.

"The deadliest animal in the world is the mosquito. What if we made a million mechanical mosquitoes?"

"That sounds itchy," Benny grimaces.

"No, I mean we make small robots that could take down a jet. They go big and we go small, over and over again."

"We have one night to get it done," Benny says. "How do we make . . ."

I jump up and snap my finger. "Remember those toy dragons you made? Were they ever destroyed?"

"I have them, but they're hard to control," Benny says. "They set the workshop on fire."

Sarah jumps up. "I'll work on a prototype. One part magic, one part mechanics. We could program them."

"That might work," he says stroking his beard.

"It's going to be a crazy night," she says.

Sarah's right. We work frantically through the night until our eyelids won't stay open anymore. When I finally head home, there are two hours left to sleep.

EIGHTEEN
ATTACK OF THE MISFITS

I wake up before sunrise. I use the term "wake up" loosely. Between the freezing bedroom (nobody bothered with a heating charm) and the upcoming attack, I barely manage a nap. I trudge over to Greg's room.

"Wake up."

He rolls over and mutters something about feeding the unicorns. "Their farts don't stink at all. They smell like peppermint, Wendell."

"Wake up," I repeat, shaking his covers.

He turns his head and says, "Just one more hour, 'kay."

So, I slap him. Not that I want to. Okay, truthfully, I don't mind slapping him. He can be a punk sometimes.

Greg grabs his wand and aims it at my throat.

"You can't go back to school today," I cough out.

"Oh, does my itty bitty baby bwudder miss me?"

"Listen, the Misfits are planning an attack and I think your chariot is one of the targets."

"Why should I believe you?"

"This is serious. You can't go. Please listen to me," I implore.

"Do you just want to make me late? Is that it? Are you looking to dishonor the family even more?"

"This is a really big deal," I point out.

"So is our family's reputation," he says, jabbing the wand closer to my throat.

"I'm sorry."

He sets his wand down and shakes his head. "I need to sleep."

As I walk away, he adds, "Turn the heat charm down in here. Oh yeah, that's right. You can't. You need magic for that."

"This is serious. I just want you to be okay."

"Can you at least shut the door? I'm trying to sleep in here," he says, pulling the covers up to his face. I stand outside his door and debate trying harder to convince him.

My stomach starts to knot, so I dart down the stairs and head out the door. Moving helps my nerves. The air is icy as I dash down the trail, past Gwynn's Galloping Unicorn Utopia and toward the Town Tetrahedron. It's quiet, aside from the snoring accordions.

I slow down to a walk as I pass by Sally's Smart Mart. A group of girls are chanting:

Wendell Darrell Dragonbooger Boy
He'd be more useful as a dragon's chew toy
He can't wield a wand and he can't do a spell
His hair is a mess and his clothes always smell
In my opinion he can go to . . .
Hello Dragonbooger, Dragonbooger
Dragonbooger Boy
You'd be more useful as a dragon toy

Big Bruno Buchanan the Ballistic Bully Boy wrote that song a few years ago and started singing it between classes last year. It took awhile, but eventually it made its way through the school and into our village.

The song really took off when his dad recorded it with a catchy guitar riff. Suddenly, the song was streaming from the phonographs in every tree house, hut and castle in the enchanted world. Even Croatian witches were dancing along. I can't really blame them. It was a catchy tune. I thought the song was over, but apparently it's making a comeback after my confession yesterday.

I march past scowling wizards patrolling the police precincts and head over to Smells Like Bundt.

Betty Bundt greets me with a tired smile, "Care for the Big Bundt Special?"

I nod.

"You've had a tough week," she says, pointing to the newspaper at the table.

"Yep."

"It gets easier. I remember when I figured out that I was a firt. It was hard. And now? I have the best pastries in all of Sweet Treat Tweet Street."

"Have you seen Benny?"

"Nope," she says as she pulls out a triple-deck, three-cream circular cake and sets it on the table.

The bells on the door jingle as Sarah whips in. Betty points to my table.

"Did you see it?" she asks.

I shake my head, clueless.

"Phil confessed to underage enchantments. Remember last night when I mentioned the unknown wizard? Well, he was the one. He took the fall for everything."

"I thought he was mad at us," I point out.

"So did I," she says.

"Besides, this ruins his chances of staying in the enchanted world."

She shrugs her shoulders.

Together we attack the Bundt cake with the energy of a hungry troll. Neither of us says much. What else is there to say? We're both too tired from last night and too anxious about today. An hour passes. Patrons stream in and order cinnamon rolls while we huddle in the corner booth.

"Benny's supposed to be here," she says.

I nod.

The sun rises and paints the steamy ground with its rays. As the minutes pass, we realize that our sitting here might be part of his plan. Send us away from the Gnome Home while Benny takes on the Misfits. All I can think about is my annoying, stubborn brother shot down by a drone.

"Maybe Benny can handle the robots all by himself. I mean, he made the originals," she points out, smashing the crumbs with her fork.

"And he has trolls," I add. "Three of them."

She shakes her head. "What if Mildred is right? What if he really is running the Misfits and we just helped him perfect his technology?"

"It's possible, but . . ."

Without warning, the door flies open. A boy in a charred-up sweatshirt stumbles in.

"Wendell . . . Sarah . . . so . . . glad . . ."

"Phil? What are you doing here?" I ask.

"Man, those zombies are a pain. You weren't joking about that."

"Wait a second, you crossed the zombie-infested catacombs?" I ask.

He nods.

"But you won't even cross the road without a crosswalk."

"Don't you want to win the contest?" Sarah asks.

"It's just a trophy. I mean, my shelf is so packed with those that I don't really need another one," he says with a nervous laugh.

His eyes light up. "Is that an accordion playing by itself?"

"It's snoring, actually. Must have snuck in here," Sarah says.

"I could get used to this place," he mutters. "I mean, I could if I was supposed to be here."

"What are you doing here?" Sarah asks. "I thought you were banned from the village."

"I don't plan on staying. But I figured it out."
He pulls the wand out from his back pocket.
"This belongs to you."

"I have one that belongs to you, too. It's from your dad," I say, pulling it out of my robe.

Tears well up in his eyes as he studies the tag.

Sarah looks at him sympathetically, "We need to talk to you about your dad."

He shakes his head. "I already know. But it's not what you think. I think he was framed."

"The evidence points . . ."

He cuts her off. "That doesn't matter right now. I figured it out. That wasn't a prophecy that Mildred said when you were born. That was a curse. I got your powers and you got my lack of powers. So, I came here to return the curse."

"That's not possible. I know Mildred. She wouldn't have cursed me."

"Just try it out. You'll see," he says. "Then you can go take on the Misfits with the magic you were always supposed to have."

"Well, thanks Phil, but I want you to keep the powers," I say, still doubting his theory.

"They won't do me any good in the DUMP," he says.

"I'll tell you what. I'll come get my powers tomorrow. How does that sound? I'm thinking today we go out and win the robotics competition," I respond. "It's not too late."

"Or we build a bigger dragon. My dad says you almost had it working," he points out.

"How did he know?" I ask.

"He said something about a cell phone. Said he planted it on you yesterday. I'm telling you, he's not who you think he is."

"If that's true, then he knows all of our plans," I point out.

"Just listen to me. He was framed."

"By Benny?"

"I don't know who framed him, but I know that he isn't in charge of the Misfits."

"We could give it a shot," I admit.

Sarah laughs. "Are you crazy? We couldn't get the wings to move. We tried electricity and magic and even duct tape."

"She's right. Besides, Benny won't let us help him today," I add.

"Wait a second. You snuck into the DUMP. You used magic when you weren't supposed to. You almost got a dragon working and now you're giving up?"

"Yeah, that's about right," Sarah says.

"No, that's not 'about right.' That's 'about wrong.' That's totally wrong, actually. Now let's get that dragon working."

He pulls me out of the chair and then pauses for a second. "Can I have a slice of that cake first?"

"Yeah. Go ahead."

He devours two slices of cake before we head over to the Gnome Home. It's open again and packed full of small patrons. I try to look casual, but my whole body is trembling.

"Can I help you?" Gnome Chomsky asks, looking up to us. "You're shivering, Wendell. You could probably use a hot butterscotch."

Sarah gives me the "go on" nod, but I'm so nervous I can't speak.

"Can I help you?" he repeats.

"Yeah, um . . ."

Sarah walks toward the backroom. "Benny forgot the needle-nose pliers," she says coolly. "We need to grab them."

I follow Sarah in. "How'd you know that Benny would be gone?"

"I knew he'd be setting up the dragon robots. The attack is less than an hour away."

"Do you really think we can defeat the jets?" I ask.

"Of course we can," Phil says. "If I learned anything from the awful Sundays spent watching football with my dad, it's that the Jets always find a way to lose."

"There are three of them," a voice says.

I look around, but don't see anyone.

"Jets, that is. There are three of them," the voice says again.

Something brushes against my ear. I jump back and turn around to see Dr. Larry Faerie the Fairy.

CHAPTER EIGHTEEN

"I tried telling that to Benny, but he didn't want to hear it. There are three jets. Unmanned drones, actually. You can take them down if you know what you're up against."

"I think we've got it covered," Sarah says, pulling up a chair behind the computer.

"I could help," he insists. "I know a thing or two about flying."

No one listens. Phil inspects the claws while I add new ball bearings to the wing joints. It makes no difference. I close my eyes and imagine Ash. She doesn't fly. She can't fly. But when she tries, she doesn't flap up and down.

"That's it. We have the movement all wrong. It's a rowing movement. Think fairy instead of eagle."

"I've seen a lot of dragons," Sarah says. "Their wings are flapping."

"Yeah, but they curve. Just trust me on this," I beg.

"We need to create a curve."

Sarah takes a deep breath and taps away at the computer, messing around with diagrams and adding new arcs. It's not working. If anything, the wings seem worse.

"I really think it's more like fairy wings," I say, staring at the screen.

Phil points to Larry. "Excuse me ma'am."

The fairy ignores him, continuing to hover over Sarah's shoulder.

"Ma'am?"

"Sir!" he whips around and growls at Phil.

"Sorry. Excuse me, sir, but can we videotape you flying."

"I suppose you could," Larry says. "My acting fee has to be negotiated with my agent. Plus, I only work with union stunt people. I suppose I could do pro bono work, but you'll need to fill out the paperwork so that I can write it off on my taxes."

"So you'll do it?" I ask.

Larry nods. Phil pulls out his phone and presses record. Larry flies around, doing a few bonus twirls just for fun.

Phil pulls out his wand, "Off from the screen and into this place, appear now before Wendell's face."

Suddenly the image drifts forward. I step up and bend the lines.

"That's it. That's how a dragon works!" I yell. I make a few minor adjustments to the wings and then Sarah does her magic. Whether it's code or spells, I have no idea. But it works. The dragon is moving its wings exactly as I sketched.

"How do we get it out?" Phil asks.

"Remove the ground without a sound. Replace it back after the attack," Sarah says.

The earth shakes as a mammoth hole appears above us.

"We don't have a remote," I point out.

"Yeah, well, you'll be controlling it from the top," Sarah says, helping me into the holster.

"Are you sure you don't want to control this?" I ask.

"You're the only one small enough to fit," Sarah says. Suddenly, I realize that she designed it for me.

"This isn't safe. There's no seatbelt," Phil complains. "How will he be able to stay . . ."

It's too late. The dragon pops up and hobbles across the street. A crowd gathers.

"It's the Misfits!" a young witch yells.

Phil sprints alongside the dragon and tosses me a phone. It bounces off my hands and lands on the dragon's neck.

"Um, I don't think I'm going to want to chat," I point out. The dragon sprints forward, flapping awkwardly, and then all-at-once, it bounds toward the sky.

I bite my lip as the earth pulls away from me. Looking down, it feels more like I'm falling than flying. I grip the cold metal neck and reach for the controllers. I pull the reins to the left. It flips sideways into a freefall. Suddenly I'm hanging upside down, hugging the dragon with a death grip. I pull the reins hard right as it twirls twice more through the air, finally ending right side up.

I loosen the grip and let it coast. Tiny specks zip below me; people, buildings, trees. I attempt a deep breath, but it doesn't happen. I'm still too nervous. Yet as the oxygen makes its way back to my brain, I focus.

For a minute time stands still. I'm floating, flying higher than any firt ever gets to fly. Then, like a snap, I know what I need to do. I head toward Pegasus Palace, the location of the send-off event for Fancy Schmancy students. A crowd of parents and students are already gathering under a floating tent.

"Please surrender!" a voice roars from behind. At least he's using "please." Technically, he doesn't have to be polite.

Over my shoulder, I spot three hooded figures on brooms. Police. One pulls out an amplified megaphone and calls out again, "Please surrender."

The phone rings. "This is kind-of a bad time to chat," I shout at phone.

"I can't believe you're getting reception," Phil says. "I love this place."

A curse pings off the metal and crackles into the wind. "Um, right now I'm not too thrilled with this place, actually."

"You're doing great," he says. "The whole village is watching." Somehow that doesn't help.

Turning toward it, I lean into the metal neck of my dragon for speed. A flash of color on a blinged-out hand alerts me that one of the hooded figures is aiming her wand at me.

Instinctively, I pull right. The dragon tailspins toward the ground. There are hoodies keeping neck and neck on either side of me. I pull up and take a hard left. The hooded wizards scream as their brooms puncture the tent. A commotion erupts inside, with witches and wizards screaming counter-deflation charms.

I glide forward and look around. Where is the drone?

A throng of miniature metal dragons pops up like tiny gnats from the forest surrounding Pegasus Palace. I follow them toward the horizon.

All at once, they swarm the oncoming drone. It tumbles down, engulfed in flames, smoke streaking through the sky.

I pull away, relieved. One down, two to go. A high-pitched curse zips past my ear. I duck again, glance back and count four wizards on brooms. A stream of fire circles around and lands on the dragon's neck. It doesn't catch but I can feel the heat through the metal.

Just get out. Pull away and explain it all to them on the ground. You haven't broken any laws.

"This is your second warning," a witch yells. "Surrender now." Okay, so they're now dropping the "please" from the instructions.

I dart down into the trees, zigzagging my way through the forest. A curse hits my forearm with a sudden jolt. I pop off the dragon, and snag the reins. I hover suspended above it with a white-knuckle grip on the reins. Numbness spreads down my arm. I wrap my legs around and slip back into the holster.

I'm heading toward a tree. I can't move my hand. Curses zip past me, pinging by my ears.

The dragon flies forward, cold metal eyes unaware of the massive oak tree ahead. There's that still awareness again, a sure knowledge that I'm about to die. Breathe in, breathe out. The faces of my family flash through my mind.

I yank the reins up with my whole arm. Suddenly I'm shooting vertical. We clear the trees and shift horizontal again.

A second drone appears, gliding above the trees. It arcs toward me. Everything happens so fast I'm not even aware of thinking. The flame cord dangles by my right rein.

Wait for it, wait for it. Now! I pull myself up by the flame cord just as the drone approaches me. A sudden burst and the drone is engulfed in flames. I pull tighter through the loud crackles.

I brace for a crash and a spectacular pyrotechnic display, but the drone only makes a smoky arc back toward the trees entangled in their tops.

I take a deep breath and look around. It's silent. It's still. I shiver. I'm high enough that if I fell, it would be the end of me. My stomach lurches and I decide not to look down again.

A curse bounces off my robot's neck. More? I turn back and wave my hands. Don't they realize that I stopped the Misfit drone?

My hand retracts. I still can't move it much. The dragon wobbles. I curl into her like a baby to his mother. We dip left as a curse zips by, grazing my face and landing in my already stiff palm. It blisters up immediately.

To my left, I see the school's carriage ascending above the trees. I pull tighter on the reins, trying to shake off the shock from the last curse. I struggle to breathe again. It's all moving too fast.

The brooms behind me drop down. A final drone arches above the carriage. Oh yeah, two down one to go. I hold my breath as I speed toward the carriage, sensing that I'm too late this time.

An ear-splitting crack. The carriage is wobbling. The drone hit them with something. My Merlin, I cannot breathe.

The figures on brooms fly back up.

Again?

We all converge on the caravan and I try to maintain a steady rhythm. The curses stop. The wizards drop down and wait for me to break with the carriage.

"It's the Misfits!" a kid yells from the carriage.

A girl waves her wand and mutters a curse. I duck, but it's pointless. She's so nervous, the curse fizzles right out the window.

"I'm not a Misfit!" I yell.

A boy looks out the window and points behind me. I steer away right as the drone approaches. It's fast and thin. I spray out a steady flame, but it dodges it instantaneously.

The carriage shakes. Two pegasae break loose, screeching like piglets as they fly away. I pull hard on the rein. The flames spew out and catch the drone's right wing this time.

I lean in for speed and pull harder on the reins. I'm gaining on the drone. I pull the flame cord again, and close my eyes. The heat is unbearable. I pull tighter, the fire singeing my arm hair.

With a loud whoosh the direction of the heat changes. I open my eyes and watch the wingless drone crash into the forest floor, snapping in two.

Wasting no time, I whip back around toward the carriage. The remaining pegasae are flapping wildly. The carriage bangs around back and forth, hanging by just a few tethers. There is some distance to cover, but I can hear my former classmates screaming.

The phone rings. "I'm kind-of busy," I point out.

"There's a ladder in the back compartment, and you can hover by lifting the reins and then dropping them real fast."

"Thanks for the heads-up," I say.

"I need to go," he says. "But you should be fine from here on out."

I follow Phil's advice. The first time I try to hover, the dragon pulls up too fast and then dives down too low. The second time, she twirls and I almost fall off the side. I try a third time and it works. But I'm far, really far, from the carriage. I reach back and lift up the compartment. A rope ladder is coiled there with one hard plank rung nested on top. It feels odd to pull a ladder out of a dragon's butt – even if the dragon is a robot dragon.

Leaning over, I stare at the ground. There's no way I'm standing up. I'm far above timberline. I shake my head.

"Dragonbooger!" a kid yells. "Toss the ladder to us."

It's Bruno.

"Just throw it!" He makes it sound so easy.

I've got one shot, but it's far.

Another rope snaps and the carriage hangs like a loose tooth, barely upright enough to keep kids from tumbling out. I count to three and launch the ladder toward the carriage window. It ricochets off the door. To my surprise, it is Sarah that reaches out and snags it.

"What are you doing here?" I shout.

"Trying to save some lives!" she yells back, before muttering a charm. I imagine it's a petrifaction charm on the dragon that I'm hugging with all my strength.

"Wendell!" she screams. "You have to come across! Go monkey style!" Easier said than done. Snap! Another rope breaks. Both pegasae strain to keep up the carriage.

"Just go!" Sarah yells. I am only a little ashamed that I whimper the whole time that I turn around in the saddle. One slip and I'm dead.

I reach out and clench the first rung on the ladder. I close my eyes and take a deep breath.

"Don't you dare!" she yells. "Keep your eyes open the whole time." I might be afraid of falling, but I'm more afraid of Sarah's wrath. I swing my feet out and lunge forward. Swing and lunge. Swing and lunge. Again and again until I'm at the last wrung. But this time I slip. A hand pulls me back. I look up. It's Bruno.

"Just trust me," he says.

I shake my head.

"Trust me," he says again, pulling on my forearm. I clutch his arm as he pulls me into the carriage. The carriage lurches as the pegasae's struggle.

Sarah points her wand at the ladder.

"I've never been madder, drop down this ladder. Now straight to the ground in one single bound." The ladder obeys, straightening up and dropping toward the ground below.

A group rushes to exit.

"Stop!" Sarah yells. "One at a time. You'll all make it. But if you rush, I swear I'll push you out."

One by one, the students climb down. The carriage sways and shakes. A few times, I feel like it's going to drop to the ground entirely. However, for all the swaying, it still manages to remain in the air.

Did you sneak on?" I ask her.

Sarah shakes her head. "I had to grovel. As if I really wanted to be in this stupid elitist academy."

"Why weren't you helping me?" I shoot back.

"Really? Do you think their aim was that bad? I was howling out a bunch of stupid counter-curses, thank you very much. The police had no idea it was me."

We wait in awkward silence as the crowd continues to climb down. Finally, Bruno, Sarah and I are the last to go.

"Where's Greg?" I ask. All of a sudden I'm frantic with the realization that I didn't see him climb out the window with the others.

Bruno shrugs. "I don't think he got on."

"No," I shake my head. "He was here. I'm sure he got on. Where is he?"

"I'm sure he's fine," Sarah says.

I shake my head. "No, that's not, no, no…" *Breathe Wendell, breathe.*

A deafening pop. The carriage slips, slamming me into the bench in front of me. I gasp and brace myself between the benches. It sways with every gesture.

"Just go, Bruno," I wheeze out.

He shakes his head. "Let Sarah go. I'll take you to the Misfits."

"How do you know?"

Snap!

The carriage wobbles. "Okay, okay. I'll go down first," Sarah says, easing onto the ladder and nimbly gliding down. I follow her, but just as I climb over the edge, snap!

The carriage tips completely sideways. I fall the rest of they way out, clutching the ladder with my blistered hands. Looking down, I see Sarah already on the ground. It's too far for me to jump. I scale the swaying ladder. Another snap. I lunge out as the carriage starts to fall. I land in a crouch only a few feet from and seconds before the crash. Debris flies over me. *I'm alive. My Merlin, I'm alive.*

Bruno!

Mr. Oglesby approaches. "Did you happen to see the metal birds they used in their attacks?"

"Bruno didn't get off," I point out. My heart is pounding. "He didn't make it."

"Well, I must say that you handled things well, Mr. Drackenberger," he says, awkwardly patting me on the back.

NINETEEN
INTO THE LAIR

As the students form lines in anticipation for a new carriage, I feel a tap on my shoulder.

"Bru—" He covers my mouth.

"Bruno, you're alive." I whisper.

He nods and points to a broom lying on the ground.

"I had a feeling I might need it," he says.

"You better hide that," I whisper. "You could get expelled for bringing a broom on the carriage."

He shakes his head.

"Why didn't you just climb down with us?"

"Because I need to buy us some time."

"They think you're dead," I point out.

"That's the plan. I grabbed a second broom for you," he says. "It's behind the parents' tent. It'll be easy. Everyone's distracted by the attacks."

"I can't ride a broom."

"Because you're a firt?"

I nod.

"Then we can ride the dragon," he says, pointing to the hovering metal creature staring at us with its cold robotic eyes.

We slip away into the forest and study the robot dragon. "We can still stop them. There's time. They won't expect it. We just . . ."

"Whoa, whoa, whoa" I interrupt. "You're telling me that there is more to their plan?"

He nods. "A kidnapping. There's no time to explain."

"Will the broom carry both of us?"

He shrugs. "Guess we'll find out."

I approach the broom timidly. The last thing I want to do right now is hold onto the kid who threw me into cauldrons. A quick kick and the broom rattles. Bruno aims it upward, but the broom bucks back and forth.

"Guess it doesn't like being a two-seater," he mutters as it bucks away from the trees and bashes me into the tent wall.

"What's going on?" a wizard yells. Bruno steers the broom up and away. My sweaty hand slips on handle.

"If we fall, they'll blame the broom. It'll be kindling for a fire," Bruno says. All at once, the broom settles down. It turns out that he can bully a broom just as well as he bullies firts.

Bruno circles back toward the crowd. "What are you doing?" I ask.

With a sudden burst, we zoom around the top of the tent, just feet above the group of students.

"Did they see me?" he asks.

"Did anyone *not* see you?"

The broom slows down as we approach the dragon.

"This is as close as we're going to get," he says.

I look down at the drop and shake my head.

"Oh, come on. You make bigger drops than this in schnorbitz. Or, I guess you don't. Anyway, it's about five feet." More like eight feet, but who's counting?

"Look, you have to go first," he says. "I'm controlling the broom."

I shake my head. The drop is too much.

"One . . . two . ." Gulp. My stomach flips as I fall, but I land squarely on the dragon and latch onto her neck. I look around. Bruno lands behind me with a clanking thud.

"You aren't going to ride your boom?" I ask.

"They'll be trailing us with brooms. They already are," he says, pointing back.

"Got it," I say, "There are hand holds for you right here." I pull on the reins. A stream of fire shoots across the sky.

"Oops. Fire cord." I pull on the reins again and hit the turbo button. The way back is faster than I anticipate, despite all the high-pitched shrieks from Bruno (which he assures me are "happy screams" and not based upon fear).

"Drop us off by Grand Stan's," he says.

"Are you crazy?"

"There's a secret passage through that little secret room thingy. You'll see."

The landing isn't perfect, with Bruno falling off before the dragon comes to a complete stop. He shrugs it off and runs toward the grandstands.

Reluctantly, I follow him to the entrance. Suddenly, it feels like a trap. What if he's delivering me to the Misfits?

"You don't trust me, do you?" he asks.

I shake my head. "Kind-of hard when you threw me into cauldrons."

"They weren't hot cauldrons," he says.

"You embarrassed me in front of the whole village."

He nods. "I know all about the Misfits. I wanted to catch you. I was so sure you were a part of them. I mean, you were buying all those smuggled parts for so long. Imagine the headlines if I had nabbed the culprit?"

"Well, I'm not. I'm not a Misfit."

"I know that now. I was wrong about that." His voice breaks off. It's the closest I'll get to an apology. He waves his wand and the corridor appears. "Just follow this all the way and you'll run into their lair."

"You're not going with me?"

"Go in and face the Misfits? That's a death wish. But you can do it. You'll be fine."

He flicks his wand and walks away. The door slams shut behind him. The phone rings in my pocket and I shriek. I'm shaking as I fumble the phone.

I hear footsteps. Heart racing, I look back at the closed door. No doorknob.

"Thought you could use some help," a voice ahead of me says. It's Charles, the brain-intolerant zombie kid.

The phone rings again. "Just leave it on with you," Phil whispers. "Don't hang up."

"Hang up?"

"Don't turn the call off. We need this for evidence."

"Where are you?" I whisper back – even though there's no one to hear me but Charles the Brain Intolerant Zombie.

"I'm in the Misfits' lair."

"Already?"

"I took off after you tossed the ladder. Sarah let me use her broom."

"Without a license?"

"I didn't think about that. But I was a safe driver, if that makes any difference." A dragon roars in the background.

"You know, I think I must have it all wrong. Are you sure they call themselves the Misfits?"

I nod.

"You there?"

I nod again. Then, remembering I'm holding a phone, I whisper, "Yeah."

"Then this is the right place. But she's sitting on a stool. Villains are supposed to have chairs with armrests. It's like Super Villain 101 or something."

"Stay there. I'm coming soon."

I follow Charles through the twirling tunnels. We snake around until we're nearly out of breath.

"I'll be waiting out here," Charles says.

"You're not going with me?" I ask.

He shakes his head. "I'm a zombie. You'd never believe it but we actually prefer peaceful resolutions. We're like Switzerland. But good luck, Wendell."

I take a deep breath and shadow box the air. *Just barge in. Go with the surprise.* I sprint toward the entrance. Before I can hit it, the door opens and I summersault through.

Mildred stands over me. "We were expecting you."

"What are you doing here? Am I in the wrong place?"

She stares at me. That's it. The rejected one, living in the tunnels, plotting revenge with items from the DUMP.

"You're a Misfit?"

"It's not too late, Wendell. We could still use your talents."

I attempt my best glare, but I'm too scared to look her in the eye.

My mind is racing to put the pieces together. "So, just because you made a bad prophecy, you want to destroy all of Bezaudorf?"

"Open your mind," she says with a grin. "It was never about the prophecy."

"Wendell!" Melissa screams from across the lair. She's chained to a chair.

"A simple charm if you could use a wand," she says. "But I don't think it's possible, is it?"

"I . . . I . . . I don't get it. Why have you been attacking the village?"

"Don't play dumb, Wendell. You know exactly why this is happening."

I think back to her story. "You did this all because you lost your fortune-telling license?"

"It wasn't just a license. It was my chance to be an equal. I want respect," she says in a cold, calculated, barely audible voice. The effect is intimidating. Stepping away from Melissa's chair, she adds, "Of all wizards, you should understand."

"It's not about the prophecy. It began when I was eight. I couldn't do magic."

"But eventually you did," I point out. "You said so yourself."

"Ahem," she clears her throat. "If you would please refrain from interrupting me as I share my emotionally scarring back-story. See, my teacher asked me to do a simple transformation. 'Turn this feather into a quill, Miss Fitz.' The kids pounced on it. They called me Mildred Misfit. They even made a song about it."

"I know how that feels," I say.

"I told you not to interrupt me. Anyhoo, I knew I had no magical powers, but this, *this* was the moment I was powerless."

"That's why you started The Misfits?"

"Exactly. It's justice for all the misfits and outcasts. And it's not all destructive. We smuggle from the DUMP. We finagle our way into the system. We have bake sales - I don't know - at least three times a year. Not quite quarterly, but not bad for a group without magic."

"I donate the cakes," Betty Bundt says from the back of the room.

"What did I say about the interruptions?" she says, shaking her head. "We've changed the laws. There was a time when a firt like you would have been sent away to the DUMP without so much as a warning."

"But you're not a firt anymore," I point out.

"Have you ever seen me use my wand? I worked hard to make things happen so that I'd be accepted as a fortune-teller. I was a member of the council and I was the only one fighting for the rights of firts," she says.

"Was Filbert a Misfit?"

"At one time, yes. He was my last apprentice. I was grooming him to take over the enterprise," she says, shaking her head.

"Benny was a Misfit too," I mutter.

"He was. And did he bother to tell you that detail? Ha! Look Wendell, we weren't violent. I mean, yes, we were destructive, but we never started off trying to kill anyone. We were trying to be disruptive. You know, helping them see that their enchanted village wasn't so perfect. However, when our lair was discovered by a couple of snooping smugglers, well, we had to take care of them. That was when Benny defected."

"You killed Sarah's parents?"

She nods. "Not on purpose. We meant to scare them, but something went horribly wrong. Benny and Filbert chickened out and told them ahead of time. The situation got severe. We had to take a few unfortunate measures."

"So Benny was a villain?"

She shakes her head, showing emotion for the first time. "We're not villains! The true villains are the wizards that demean the firts and the rejects. The true enemy is the kid who threw you into cauldrons. Think about it. Notice how many wizards we've killed since then."

"But you destroyed the library," I point out. "And you destroyed half of the Town Tetrahedron. You ruined people's lives."

She laughs. "Sweet, naïve Wendell. Think of it this way: they experienced for a day what you have experienced your whole life. Even then, they hardly experienced any pain. They got sympathy instead of ridicule. They just magic things back into place instead of having to work hard to fix what was broken. Today was supposed to be different. And it can be. We'll rebuild."

Suddenly I realize that she wins regardless of what happens. If I fail to stop her, she takes over the village. But if I stop her, I become the hero and her prophecy comes true. I can tell the truth, but who's going to believe me? I've already told so many lies that even my family doesn't trust me.

I step toward the door. She smiles. "It's self-locking. Unless you have the key, you don't get out." She points to a dragon. "Chances are you don't want to wrestle him for it, either. Besides, you wouldn't walk away from your sister, would you?"

Where are Phil and Sarah? Why aren't they jumping in to help? My mind races with ideas. I could get the dragon to catch the door on fire and then . . . I'd die in the process. I could pretend to join the Misfits and then . . . they would keep an eye on me the whole time.

I glance at the shadows where Phil tiptoes toward my sister's chair. There have to be ten or eleven guards right there, plus the dragons.

I pull out the wand that Filbert gave me. Mildred laughs. "Yes, I'm sure it's going to work right now."

"Actually, it will. See, I met Filbert Junior. You know, the kid you had me find. And he said a rhyme, a counter-curse I guess, and now I have his powers. Or was that . . . was that supposed to happen tomorrow? Right, I become magical after I'm the hero? Was that how the plan was supposed to work?"

Her face drops. "That's impossible. I can't do magic. How could I do a curse?"

I aim my wand at her throat. "You want to test it?"

She whips out a wand and mutters an unintelligible Latin phrase. Suddenly a sharp pain shoots up my arm. All around, the guards mumble and mutter. Phil jumps from the shadows and points his wand at the chair. "Let the chains drop and . . ."

Mildred spins around. Sparks fly. Phil screams. Sarah barges through the door, startling a dragon. She dodges a stream of fire, pulls out a snow-cone cannon and smiles. Suddenly the place is packed with steam. Guards are running and arguing, but Mildred remains calm.

"This is insane! Drop each chain!" Phil yells from the ground. One by one, the chains unhinge. My sister wriggles loose. Two more dragons gather near Sarah, both spewing fire. It's too much for the cannon. The room echoes with pops and sizzles, and I can hardly see through the steam.

No magic. No machines. I'm powerless. But then the story of the Stinky Flower and the Ninjas pops into my head. That's it. The dragons have a super-sensitive sense of smell.

As Sarah and Mildred fire curses back and forth, I pull a few of Benny's marker's from my pocket; Fresh Flatulence. I have five of them. The smell wafts through the air as one by one, the dragons whine.

"Wendell? What did you eat?" Sarah yells.

Ug Lee shakes his head and lets out a hideous howl. I tiptoe toward him, closing my eyes as I approach his trunk-like neck. Standing up on his hind legs, he howls again. With my ears ringing and my pulse pumping, I jump up and yank on his collar. He pulls his head back and chomps down, ripping my shirt just above my wrist.

With my left hand, I twist the key ring. Slowly, it shifts and the key begins to slip. With a sudden jolt, he pulls back again, sending me airborne toward the wall. The key hits the ground as Ug returns to all fours. I look down. It's under his front claw.

A curse blazes past my chin. Turning back, I look at the far corner. The door bursts open. It's my grandma, saddled on a runt of a gray dragon. It can't be. It is. My grandma is riding Ash.

"Here girl!" I yell.

Tail wagging, she hops forward. Ug twirls around and bashes the dragon's head against the wall with his spiked tail. She lets out a yelp and cowers. I crawl below him and snatch the key. Three more markers fall out so I open them for good measure; vomit this time.

Betty Bundt decides to join the fray and rushes Ug's side like a champion cow-tipper.

"You're on our side?" I ask.

"Always have been," she grins.

Ash dodges to the left as Ug tumbles into the wall. A bookcase falls over. He shakes his head and pops back up. He bounds toward my dragon. I need a distraction.

"Over here!" I yell.

Nothing.

I jump toward him and pull out the roll of pegasus stickers. They prance off the page and gallop toward the dragon. Ug sticks his forked tongue out and wags his tail. I uncap a final marker as he lunges toward me. The scent is too much.

Ug Lee howls again and cowers in the corner. Melissa steps up onto Ash's back.

"Greg's waiting outside," grandma says. "He can guide Ash back home."

"He's alive. Greg made it out alive?"

"He never left in the first place." She smiles. "He may not listen to his brother, but he listens to his grandma."

"Come on, Ash," I coax her toward the door. Who knows how long the smell will keep the other dragons distracted? Timidly, she steps toward the door. I twist the key. Ash looks out door and ducks.

"Go on, girl," I implore. She backs up.

Slow Lee spews a stream of fire, barely missing the doorway. Ash stumbles forward, ducks out the door and flies through the graveyard.

Sarah reaches for her satchel. A curse from Mildred ricochets off the wall and lacerates her leg.

"Agh!" she screams.

"Go, go!" I shout to her. "I'll catch up."

I snag the snow cone machine from her and press the button right as two dragons spew flames. The room fills with steam.

"Where's Phil?" I call over my shoulder.

Sarah hesitates, shakes her head in confusion, and then shrugs. "He said he had to use the restroom."

I face forward again and realize that the dragons have backed off and I'm still spraying snow at no one.

The room is empty. My grandma and Betty Bundt have chased off the remaining guards, along with the dragons. I stand alert, uncertain of what to expect.

"Let's go, Wendell," Sarah says.

"The mist thing worked out perfectly."

"Well, I stole that idea from the robot fair," she stepping out the door.

The door slams shut. A figure emerges from the mist. It's Mildred. She pulls her wand out and aims it at my chest.

"With this spell, I take your breath. When it's done, you'll face your death."

I fall back choking. I can't breathe. My heart races. My head is light. Things blur. Mildred stares into my eyes, holding the wand with a steady hand. In the distance, I can hear a pounding on the door. This is it. I won't make. Blood rushes to my face. My neck tightens.

From the corner of my eye, Phil sprints toward me. He slides in front of me with a mirror.

She drops her wand and clutches her throat. It's no use. The mirror continues the curse.

I gasp for breath behind Phil, and turn away. I look back at Mildred. Our eyes meet and I see her as a person. I know what she's done, but I also see her giving me Ash Lee and helping me pick out robot parts from her collection.

"Phil, you have let her live."

He shakes his head. "No."

"You have to stop this," I demand. But he's holding steady.

"Phil, stop!"

"No," he mutters. "She's getting what she dished out."

"Phil, stop!" I shout. I grab the mirror from him and shatter it on the ground.

Mildred falls to her hand and knees, wheezing through great hideous gulps as she labors to make her lungs work again.

Sarah bursts through the door behind us.

"You let her live?" Sarah asks.

All I can manage is a nod. We walk through her lair, eyes on Mildred's pathetic form. We back into the catacombs as Zombies surround us waving their torches and mumbling. I close my eyes and brace for the worst, but they don't stop. Instead, one by one, they file into her lair.

"That's the culprit," Charles says, pointing toward the door. Mr. Oglesby nods and mouths out a "thank you."

"Are they going to eat her brains?" Phil asks.

"No, but they'll certainly mess with her mind. It'll be an interesting trip to jail."

TWENTY
BRING YOUR DRAGON
TO WORK DAY

It's the next morning and I'm feeling like a giant at the tiny table of the Gnome Home. It's a fitting feeling after yesterday. Apparently, the phone recorded everything that happened.

Benny saunters over and hands me a mug of hot butterscotch. My hands are sore, even after a trip to the apothecary.

"I'm surprised you're not part of the celebrations," he says.

"I'm your apprentice. I figured you'd have some yards for me to clean up or something."

In the distance, they're playing a song about me. Instead of being a dragon's chew toy, this time it's remade so that I'm "the one that doesn't quit. He can stop any Misfit."

CHAPTER TWENTY

I take a sip just in time to prevent a flying scrap of parchment from landing in it. I watch it from over the rim of my mug, fluttering like a butterfly. It lands on my shoulder. Carefully, I unfold it.

Dear Mr. Drackenberger,
    You are cordially granted admission into Fancy Shmancy Magical Academy for Great and Awesome and Even Occasionally Terrible Wizards.
    This note hereby stands as an official invitation. Should you choose to accept, please send back a reply by week's end. The carriage has been repaired. Furthermore, Dean, the Dean of Students, is eager for a private reception in your honor.
    We understand that you have some limitations. However, we will modify our curriculum to meet your exceptional talents. Should you choose to accept this invitation, we would like to offer you the opportunity to give the opening address to all students.
                    Sincerely,
                    The Admissions Team

I fold the note and place it in my pocket.

"Who was that from?" Benny asks.

"Just a congratulations letter."

The door bursts open. Phil jumps down the stairs behind a puff of smoke and camera flashes.

"I'm off the hook," he announces.

"They're not pressing charges?"

"Turns out you can use magic if you're from the DUMP if you don't know any better. Remember what Sarah said about it?"

"What about the broom ride?"

"That'll be our secret," he says with a smile.

Benny turns around and chucks his mug at the wall.

"What was that for?" Phil asks.

"It's disposable," Benny says. Then pointing to the wall, he adds, "but it's okay. This is the kind that can be recycled."

Phil marvels at the pieces floating up and reassembling into a new mug.

"Does it always do that?" he asks.

"Yeah, I guess," I mumble.

Phil shakes his head. "I have so much to learn." He pulls out an envelope and points to my letter.

"It looks like we're going to be classmates."

Benny tries his best to offer a smile.

"Actually, I've already started an apprenticeship. But don't worry. You'll make new friends."

CHAPTER TWENTY

"Sarah's going to be there," he says.

"But her parents..."

"Are finally gone. That was the unfinished business they had to take care of. She hung out with them this morning."

"I was going to stop by and see her, but I get it if she wants to be alone." I say.

"No, she's out celebrating. Her parents are finally in a better place and she's ... relieved. I don't get it, but that's Sarah."

Benny climbs up on the table and pats me on the back. "I think you should go to the academy."

I imagine myself at the front row of the carriage. Kids would ask for the details and I would say, "You'll have to read the book." I'd hand them the book you're reading right now and wait for them to ask for an autograph.

Maybe I could stand before the throngs of students offering the opening address, talking about the rights of misfits and the need for more options in our community.

But I don't go to the Fancy Shmancy Magical Academy for Great and Awesome and Even Occasionally Terrible Wizards. Instead, I choose to continue with Benny. We start a company called Firt Assistance, Resources and Technology, or FART for short.

We plan to make stuff for firts, so they don't feel disenchanted. My first idea is a device that knocks over a door if it doesn't have a handle. Or maybe a doorbell. I haven't decided yet.

Our shop is being built at the newly refurbished Town Tetrahedron, but we plan to do most of our real work in the former Misfit lair while Filbert the Firt mans the shop.

The Council is letting us keep Mildred's Lair as long as we take care of her dragons. Which is nice, because it means every day is Bring Your Dragon to Work Day. How many jobs let you do that? The shop isn't not far from Smell's Like Bundt, where Betty has offered me free hot butterscotch for the rest of my life.

So, that's the official story. That's the one you'll read in the *Wizarding Word*. However, there's a tad bit more than what most magic folk know. The Council of Counsel thinks I did such a great job finding Phil that they want me to work on secret missions to find wizards who are stranded in the DUMP.

You know, the first time I stepped foot in the DUMP, I thought it was enchanted. I couldn't begin to understand what caused a car to move forward. I thought that Phil's phone was magical. I thought the microphone was magical. I thought all of it was magical.

I was right.

Magic is all around if I'm willing to see it.

Printed in Great Britain
by Amazon